THE YELLOW FEATHER MYSTERY

The HARDY BOYS *Mystery Stories*
BY FRANKLIN W. DIXON

Frank inserted the document in the secret hiding place

Frank inserted the document in the secret hiding place

THE YELLOW FEATHER MYSTERY

BY

FRANKLIN W. DIXON

NEW YORK
GROSSET & DUNLAP
Publishers

CONTENTS

CHAPTER I

A Strange Request

SKATING against the stiff evening wind, Frank and Joe Hardy streaked across the frozen surface of Willow River toward Woodson Academy. The bright winter moon was rising beyond the big square buildings that loomed on their right along the sloping riverbank.

"Why do you suppose Gregory Woodson phoned us to meet him at the school boathouse?" Joe asked his brother.

"Just before the connection was broken, Greg said he feared that someone might overhear us in the dormitory," Frank replied. "I guess what he's going to tell us must be top secret."

"It sure sounds so," Joe remarked as the boys approached the meeting place. "Well, he ought to be here. It's five-thirty."

Dark-haired Frank Hardy, eighteen, and his blond brother, a year younger, were known in Bay-

1

port, where they lived, as clever amateur detectives. Although they were still high school students, they often helped their father, a nationally famous sleuth, solve baffling cases. Occasionally they were asked to solve a mystery on their own, like the present one.

Joe reached the boathouse raft a few feet ahead of Frank. His brother skated in behind him and stopped short.

The building was pitch black and the silence intense. Suddenly from only a few feet away a youthful voice called to them quietly:

"Come straight across the float, fellows. I'm right in front of you!"

"Is that you, Woodson?" Frank asked.

"Yes, it is. You're the Hardys?"

"That's right."

As the boys walked forward on their skates, a tall, slender young man moved out of the shadows. The Hardys judged him to be about twenty-two years old.

"I'm sorry we were interrupted when you phoned," Frank began. "You want us to help you solve a mystery?"

"Yes, I need help badly. My grandfather, Elias Woodson, was headmaster and owner of the Academy until his recent death. It's about him and the inheritance I'm supposed to receive that I'd like to talk to you."

Both Hardy boys immediately warmed up to the pleasant young man and Joe said, "Dad's an alumnus of the Academy and knew your grandfather well. I'm sure Dad would want us to help you."

"Thanks," Woodson responded. "I'm glad you'll take the case—you might call it the mystery of the Yellow Feather."

"Yellow Feather?" Joe repeated.

"I'll explain in a moment," Woodson replied. "I have a key to the boathouse. Let's go inside out of the wind and I'll show you a clue I brought along."

Frank followed him. As Joe was about to enter the building, a wild scream out on the river arrested their attention.

"Look there!" he cried.

A short distance down the shore several students were skating near a large bonfire. Close by a large black hole yawned in the ice. Joe caught sight of a young boy trying to crawl back from the thin-surfaced area at the edge of it.

Joe did not wait. Like a flash he was off across the ice, with Frank and Greg trailing him. As Joe approached, the youngster shrieked in terror, crashed through the ice, and disappeared. There were cries of horror from his companions.

Quickly Joe unlaced his shoes, kicked them off, and without hesitation slid into the dark water. As Greg Woodson and Frank looked on, ready to help, he rose to the surface with the struggling boy.

"Hold on!" Frank cried.

He had spotted a long heavy log in a woodpile near the bonfire. Grabbing one end of it, he asked

Greg to help him and together they laid the log across the thin ice and the hole. While they held the log, Joe pulled himself and the young skater up on it and slowly they made their way to a safe spot on firm ice.

Immediately the rescued twelve-year-old began to shake from the shock of the icy water. His young friends crowded around in awe and fright, explaining to the Hardys that they had been playing snap-the-whip when their end player, Skinny Mason, had been flung off over the ice.

"You okay, Skinny?" one of the players asked.

"I—I g-guess so."

Frank whipped off his heavy leather jacket and wrapped it around the shivering lad.

"Th-thanks," Skinny quavered. "I'll b-be all r-r-right now." He looked gratefully at Joe and added, "I-I'll never forget you s-saved my l-life!"

In reply, Joe gave the boy a friendly pat on the shoulder as Greg put his skating jacket on the dripping rescuer.

"Come on. We'd better get you both to the school," he said.

An older boy skated up, saying that he would take charge of Skinny. As he moved off with the youngster, Joe turned to Greg Woodson.

"Is there any place we can go except the main school building where I can dry my clothes? I want to hear the rest of your story."

Greg thought a moment. "I know just the place—

the caretaker's cottage. It's not far. Nobody will be there at this hour. The door's always open and I know the Teevans well. They've been here a long time."

Reaching the snow-covered riverbank, the boys removed their skates and hurried through a patch of woods to the Teevan cottage. A low light shone inside. As Greg had predicted, the couple were not at home. As he opened the door and invited them to enter, Greg remarked that the Teevans held open house for anyone who wanted to stop in.

"Students do it often," he explained. "They like to raid Mrs. Teevan's refrigerator. She's the cook at school and brings leftovers down here."

A few minutes later the three were seated in comfortable chairs before an open fire. Joe had wrapped Mr. Teevan's bathrobe about him while his clothes dried in front of the blaze. Greg had made hot cocoa for all of them.

"Okay," Frank said as he sipped the steaming drink. "Tell us your story, Greg."

"The day before Grandfather's death," he began, "I received a phone call from him at Myles College, where I'm a student. It was pretty weird. He told me that his health was failing rapidly, and he wanted to tell me about the Yellow Feather."

The Hardys moved closer to Woodson.

"I never did find out what he meant," the young man continued. "Grandfather suddenly became ill and hung up. The next day I received a call from

Henry Kurt, the assistant headmaster, telling me my grandfather had died."

"That's too bad," the Hardys said sympathetically in unison, and Frank added, "How long ago was this?"

"Several weeks," Greg replied. "So far no will has been found." He paused, then added, "Grandfather told me that under his will I was to receive his entire estate."

Frank raised his eyebrows. "Has a thorough search been made?"

"Oh, yes. When the will was not found in the usual places, I tested all the walls at the school for secret panels and hidden closets. But now I have a new worry. Since I've been here searching, I've received several mysterious phone calls and a couple of unsigned letters warning me to leave Woodson Academy before I get into trouble. I think the person is the Yellow Feather!"

The Hardys looked at each other, perplexed.

"It's a mighty queer name for anyone unless he's an Indian," Joe commented. "Have you any clues to his identity? You mentioned something at the boathouse."

"I never thought of a certain peculiar letter as a clue to the mystery until this afternoon," Greg answered. "Just a couple of days after Grandfather's death, I received it in the mail.

"Grandfather had addressed the envelope," Greg continued. "I'm sure of that, even though the ink was nearly washed off. Inside the envelope was a sheet of white paper with the name *Hardy* printed in the top left corner."

"Yes?" Frank prodded, startled to hear that his own family might be involved in the mystery.

"That was the only writing on the sheet," Greg explained. "But below the name was something most unusual—a group of small rectangular cutouts arranged horizontally. Here, I'll show it to you."

Greg crossed the room to where his jacket hung over a chair. He ran his hands through the pockets, at first slowly, then with frantic speed. At last he wheeled about, his face ash white.

"The paper—and the envelope—I've lost them!" he groaned.

CHAPTER II

A Gimmick on Ice

AT THE Hardys' suggestion Greg Woodson made a search of all his pockets for the missing envelope. But it was of no avail.

"That piece of paper might be the key to the mystery of the Yellow Feather!" he said.

"Perhaps you dropped the envelope when we were rescuing Skinny," Joe suggested.

Greg snapped his fingers. "Of course I did. I remember feeling the envelope in my pocket when we started toward Skinny Mason. It must have slipped out."

"Let's take a look," Frank proposed, jumping up.

Since Joe's clothes were now completely dry, he quickly donned them so that he could go along. Greg borrowed two flashlights from the kitchen closet, then the three boys grabbed their skates and hurried from the cottage. At the river's edge they sat down to put on their skating shoes. As Greg struggled with a broken lace, he said, "I'd hoped to become Grandfather's assistant here after I graduate from college in June. Then when he died, I figured on running the school myself."

"But until a will is found you can't do that, I suppose," Frank said.

"That's right. But it won't be easy to run the school even so. It has been struggling to keep going for several years."

"Dad has mentioned that the enrollment's fallen off," Joe spoke up.

"But with certain new ideas I have, I believe it would pick up again," Greg answered. Then he added, "I'm afraid the Yellow Feather is in some way responsible for the missing will. That's why it's so important to find him."

By this time all three had their skates on and started swiftly down the river. Fanning out with the two borrowed flashlights and the one Frank carried in his pocket, they searched from the boathouse all the way to the scene of Skinny Mason's mishap.

"No sign of the envelope here," Joe called from one side of the river.

There were disappointed responses from Frank in the middle and Greg on the other wing.

Refusing to give up, they scanned the riverbank, thinking the wind might have blown the letter up on the shore. But there was no sign of it.

"I'll come back here first thing in the morning,"

Greg announced with determination. "That letter must be around somewhere and I'm going to find it!"

The boys skated out to the middle of the river. Frank was about to suggest that he and Joe start for home and return in the morning when they heard the noise of a motor.

"Where's that coming from?" Greg asked.

A buzzing sound, which grew louder each second, seemed to be moving up the river.

"Sounds like a giant bumblebee!" Joe said laughingly.

As the boys peered curiously toward a bend in the river, waving their flashlights, Frank shouted, "Hey, look out!"

With a shove, he sent Greg and Joe sprawling to one side. As he did, a shadowy bulk bore down on them and whisked past in the darkness.

"Wow!" Joe exclaimed. "What kind of iceboat was that?"

"I don't know, but did you feel the backwash?" Frank exclaimed. "It felt like one from a small plane."

Before the others could answer his question, Frank gave another cry of warning.

"Look out! Here it comes back!"

But this time the iceboat was moving slowly. Just before it reached them it scraped to a complete stop.

"Hi, fellows! Thought I recognized your voices."

"Chet—Chet Morton!" the Hardys cried.

"What kind of gimmick is that you're running?" Joe asked. "You scared me out of a night's sleep."

"I stayed up all night myself putting it together," said Chet as he hopped from the weird contraption, which looked like a cross between a bobsled and an iceboat.

The Hardys' chubby friend had become well acquainted with mystery and danger when he had been involved with them some time before in unraveling the secret of *The Tower Treasure*. And in the boys' latest case he had risked his life with theirs to solve the mystery of *The Crisscross Shadow*.

Reaching the boys, Chet said, "I sure didn't mean to come so close, but I couldn't see very far ahead. Besides, the rudder on this thing's not working so well."

Frank introduced the pug-nosed, freckle-faced Chet to Greg, then examined the strange-looking craft as well as he could with his flashlight.

"No sail," he observed. "But you certainly were moving along, Chet. Say—what's this, a propeller back here? Of course it is!"

"Like a catamaran," Joe cried, "but for travel on ice. It's a pretty swell idea."

Proudly Chet admitted to being the inventor.

"Not only for ice," he corrected Joe, "but for snow. It has interchangeable skis and skate blades, too."

Greg was impressed and said so. "I saw a lot of that sort of thing on the shallow canals when I was touring the South a couple of years ago. But I never thought of using one this way."

"It works fine," Chet told him. "That is, it did until I had to run clear up on the riverbank to miss that old sourpuss back there."

"What old sourpuss?" Frank queried.

"Oh, I was moving along pretty well when some guy on skates crossed right in front of me. I almost turned myself inside out to avoid hitting him."

Chet pointed to the rudder, which was bent out of position.

"And then he had the nerve to bawl me out," the boy complained. "I thought he'd shake his goatee right off onto the ice."

Greg started. "You say he wore a goatee? Was he a man in his late thirties?" When Chet nodded, Greg said, "That must have been Henry Kurt, the assistant headmaster I was telling you fellows about. The court appointed him to be in charge of the school until the year's over."

"He looked more like an absent-minded professor to me than a headmaster," Chet remarked. "Skating along, trying to read some piece of paper by flashlight, instead of watching where he was going."

Greg and the Hardys looked at one another, the same thought in each one's mind. Could Kurt have picked up the missing letter?

There was no answering that question now, the Hardys knew, but they would certainly try to find out later. After a few minutes' further conversation,

Greg excused himself to return to the Academy, saying he would see the boys in the morning.

"Sure thing," they agreed.

After Greg had left, Frank said, "Let's get this phantom racer of Chet's started and head back to Bayport."

"Yes, crank her up, Chet," Joe demanded. "You can tow us all the way to town—and a late supper."

But when their stout friend attempted to spin the flywheel of the small motor which ran the craft's propeller, there was no response. Grunting from the exertion, Chet tried again and again to start the motor.

"Something's wrong!" he wailed. "It won't catch! Well," he added with a resigned sigh, "I guess you fellows will have to tow *me* home."

"What!" Joe cried. "We can't drag that thing five miles to Bayport. It would take all night."

Fighting off the temptation to tease the worried Chet with a suggestion that the prized propeller sled be left standing right where it was, Frank offered the only possible solution.

"Biff Hooper's folks have a summer place up here, you know. We can pull your gimmick over to their dock, Chet, and tie it up for tonight. Tomorrow you can come back and do a repair job."

"Okay," Chet agreed. "But you'll have to help me."

It took only a few minutes to find the Hooper camp. After Chet had lashed his craft to the dock, he put on the skates he had brought along and the trio headed for Bayport.

It was well past the usual dinner hour at the Hardy home when the brothers trotted up the front steps. Mrs. Hardy met them at the door.

"Oh, I'm so glad you're home!" cried their mother, a slim, pretty woman, who had been watching anxiously for her sons. As they hugged her close and teased her gently for worrying about them, she added, "I always wonder about that river."

Joe patted her shoulder and laughed. "That river, that car, that football field—oh, Mother, you have so many worries about the places we go!"

"And don't we always come back in fine shape?" Frank asked good-naturedly.

A new voice, pleasant but firm, broke in, "*You* may have, but your clothes haven't! Joe, yours look like a burlap sack! Own up now. You got soaked. What's the story?"

The speaker was tall Aunt Gertrude, who, like her brother Fenton Hardy, enjoyed unraveling mysteries, but she had her own peculiar ways of doing so. And she liked nothing better than to chide her nephews when she suspected that they were trying to hide something. Despite this they loved and admired her.

Before the brothers could explain the reason for Joe's appearance, a deep male voice boomed out, "Well, boys, you look as if you'd been sleuthing in a shower room!"

Fenton Hardy, their tall, dark-haired father, smiled broadly as he came downstairs. "Come on, let's eat! You fellows have been holding up dinner and I have to catch a train."

"We're sorry, Dad, but we have a good excuse," Joe spoke up.

"We'll explain about our new mystery at the table," Frank promised.

During the hearty meal of steak, baked potatoes, and apple pie, Frank and Joe told of rescuing Skinny, then of their meeting with Greg Woodson and his theory about the Yellow Feather.

As they finished, Mr. Hardy's eyes were twinkling. Reaching into one of his pockets, the detective drew out a sheet of white paper.

"Look at this, boys," he said, holding it up.

In the upper left-hand corner the name *Hardy* had been printed by hand. Below it were a series of rectangular cutouts!

Both boys stared dumfounded, then cried out, "Where'd that come from?"

"Henry Kurt, the headmaster of Woodson Academy. He brought it to me a little while ago," the detective explained.

"What!" the boys shouted.

"Kurt," Mr. Hardy went on, "wants *me* to solve the mystery of the Yellow Feather!"

CHAPTER III

A Three-cornered Puzzle

"KURT asked you to solve the mystery of the Yellow Feather?" Frank gasped.

"Yes," Mr. Hardy replied. "He left here just a short time before you arrived. He had a pair of skates tucked under his arm—must have skated down from the school."

The boys nodded in astonishment and Joe asked breathlessly, "Did he say where he got the paper?"

The detective shook his head. "No, that never came up. He simply asked me to help solve the mystery of the Yellow Feather. I told him I was leaving town for a week—that I'd help him when I returned. He gave me the sheet of paper and urged that I get on the case as soon as possible."

"Same thing Greg asked us," Frank said. "Are you going to do it, Dad?"

Mr. Hardy smiled. "Yes, I am—that is, if you

don't solve it before I get back. It's too bad I can't start work right now, but my train leaves in less than an hour."

"You seem really concerned, Dad," Joe observed.

"Why shouldn't I be?" Mr. Hardy retorted. "Woodson Academy's my own school."

A sudden light gleamed in Joe's eyes. "Why don't we join forces?"

"You mean tell Kurt?" his father asked. "I'm afraid that he wouldn't welcome any help from fellows as young as you. Excited as Kurt was about his problem, he didn't seem to express much confidence in me."

"But you said the school needs help!" Frank urged.

"That's true," Mr. Hardy said thoughtfully. "And I see no reason why we couldn't combine our sleuthing. You can start on the case while I'm away."

The boys beamed their approval.

"Before I leave, though," the detective promised, "I'll get off a wire to a friend of mine in the FBI, asking if they have any listing of a criminal known as the Yellow Feather. That might give you fellows a lead."

"In the meantime, we can start work on finding out who he is," Frank said with assurance.

"And also the significance of the sheet of paper with the cutouts," Joe added.

"But remember," their father said, "the courts will take care of the legal aspects of the inheritance, pending the appearance of a will. You won't have to bother your heads about that."

It was decided that Frank and Joe on their visit to the Academy the following day would inform Greg Woodson and Henry Kurt of the Hardys' decision to work simultaneously on both requests.

"We'd better call Chet and tell him we'll have to break our date," Frank reminded his brother.

"I'll do it," Joe offered and went to the telephone.

Next morning, as the Hardys sped along in their convertible with Frank at the wheel, they discussed the possibilities of what might happen at the school.

"I wonder how Greg and Kurt will take the news," Joe remarked.

"It's my guess that Greg will be a good sport about it," Frank replied. "But not Kurt. If he's as much of a sourpuss as they say, we may have trouble with him."

"We know Greg's story," said Joe. "Let's tackle Kurt first and see what he has to say."

"Good idea."

Reaching the grounds of Woodson Academy, Frank turned into the winding driveway. Ahead of them in the snow-covered landscape stood a long colonial-type brick building partially covered with ivy. From it rose a circular bell tower. Scattered about were smaller, newer structures.

Frank pulled up in front of the main entrance and parked. The boys hopped out.

"We'd better start by asking for Kurt," Frank suggested.

A student just coming out of the building gave directions to the headmaster's office. It was a few doors down the long corridor which adjoined the entrance hall.

Frank knocked on the door and it was opened by a slender, graying man, who carried himself very erect, with an almost military bearing. His dark eyes were keen and he wore a well-trimmed pointed goatee.

As soon as introductions had been exchanged, Henry Kurt said crisply, "Have you boys brought me a message from your father?"

"Yes. He asked us to speak to you and Greg Woodson together," Frank replied.

"Greg and me? Together?"

"Yes," Frank answered. "We find you're both interested in the same mystery and have the identical problem."

A trace of annoyance crossed the man's face but he did not show as much surprise as they had expected. He cleared his throat and said:

"Umph! Well, if that's what your father wants . . . certainly. Just a moment."

He left the office and the brothers could hear him sending a messenger to the Academy's guest room in quest of Greg. When Kurt returned he seated himself at his desk, then said:

"I understand that your father is an alumnus of our school."

"He is," Frank replied. "And he's very much concerned about what happens to Woodson Academy."

"Naturally," Kurt remarked. "That's why I believe we can work together to solve this mystery."

It took only a few minutes for Greg Woodson to join them. The young man looked puzzled to see the Hardys there but greeted them pleasantly. Frank, as spokesman, explained the boys' mission. Both Kurt and Greg expressed amazement and showed an immediate antagonism toward each other.

"It's a strange coincidence," Frank commented.

Kurt fingered his goatee nervously, while Greg looked to Frank for more information.

"Dad's been called out of town," Frank went on, "and has asked Joe and me to help both of you while he's away."

Kurt jerked to his feet, an angry look on his face.

"Help me? Young boys like you? What do you think you can do about delving into the criminal activities of someone we don't even know?"

"We've done a lot of detective work, Mr. Kurt," Joe said quickly. "With our father, and without him, too."

The headmaster looked uncomfortable. To break the tension, Greg said, "It's all right with me if Frank and Joe work for both of us. The quicker this mystery is solved the better."

Kurt surveyed the brothers icily, but finally he

said in a flat tone, "I suppose if your father thinks you're capable of handling an affair as important as this I'll have to trust his judgment."

"Dad knows what he's doing, Mr. Kurt," Frank replied. "Don't be concerned about that. Now, would you mind clearing up one point?"

"What is it?"

"We've been wondering where you got the sheet of paper you left with Dad last night—the one with the rectangular cutouts."

For a second the headmaster simply stared at them without answering.

"Did you find it on the ice yesterday?" Joe asked impulsively.

"Of course not!" Kurt exclaimed. "That letter was given to me personally by Mr. Elias Woodson just before he died. But he didn't have time to tell me what the cutouts meant. So I took it to your father to decipher."

"Why did you wait so long?" Joe asked.

"I've been busy reorganizing the school," Kurt reminded them. "I want to talk to you boys alone. Greg, would you please step outside?"

The young college student looked annoyed but left the office. As soon as he had closed the door behind him, Kurt leaned forward confidentially.

"I thought it best not to upset Greg about what I'm going to tell you," he said. "Greg's a nice enough fellow personally, but he has no head for business. His grandfather knew that. At one time

Elias Woodson planned to leave the school to him but was forced to change his mind."

The Hardys were astonished at the statement. This certainly complicated matters.

"When did Elias Woodson change his mind?" Frank asked.

"Oh, I don't know exactly," Kurt answered. "But soon after I'd come to the school, he recognized my ability and decided to bequeath it to me."

Frank and Joe looked at each other. A feeling of distrust and resentment toward this braggart was building up in their minds.

"I'm worried about two things," Kurt continued. "First, the will of Elias Woodson has not been found. This hampers my efforts. And second, a mysterious character who uses a yellow feather as an insigne constantly threatened old Mr. Woodson and now me with both bodily harm and the burning of the school. Recently he sent me notes claiming that the school property rightfully belongs to him!"

"This makes a three-cornered puzzle," Frank thought. He kept silent, however, as did Joe, waiting for Kurt to continue.

"Of course," the headmaster went on, "the Yellow Feather's claim is a lot of nonsense, because I know that Elias was an assistant to his own father over fifty years ago. The school's been in the Woodson family for a century."

As the boys listened intently to every word, they

hoped that the school would not go out of the Woodson family.

"One more thing," Kurt said. "I have filed application to become administrator of the estate since there is practically nothing in it but the school."

"How do you know that, Mr. Kurt?" Frank asked.

"From Elias Woodson himself," the headmaster quickly replied.

Frank and Joe looked quizzically at each other. Greg Woodson would not be happy to hear of this development!

"You may call Greg in now," Kurt said. "Tell him whatever you think best."

Joe went to get Greg, who returned and said to Kurt, "I think I'd prefer to talk to the Hardys alone, too. Frank and Joe, will you come to my room?"

"That seems fair enough," Frank agreed. He and Joe excused themselves and left Kurt scowling.

The two youths went upstairs with Woodson to the school's guest room. It was located in the center of the building among the students' rooms. Greg closed the door and the three sat down to discuss the problem.

"Greg," Frank began, "how long before your grandfather died did he mention willing you the school?"

"At Christmas time. He spent the day with me. Why?"

"Because two other people are claiming the place belongs to them," Frank replied.

"What!" Greg exclaimed. "Who are they?"

"Kurt himself and the Yellow Feather!"

Greg's face whitened, then as the color returned he almost shouted, "The nerve of them! Woodson Academy belongs to me!"

Frank explained what Kurt had told him and Joe, adding that it now was imperative that they find Elias Woodson's will, and also locate the Yellow Feather.

"It's going to be mighty uncomfortable staying here under the circumstances," Greg remarked. "But Kurt can't keep me away when I want to come!"

"He won't be easy to get along with," Joe prophesied. "Is he popular with the students?"

"He's a strict disciplinarian, the boys tell me," Greg replied. "He has his favorites, and most of the students know it. He spends a lot of time playing around with various inventions, too."

"Inventions!" Joe exclaimed.

"Oh, he's a whiz at spring propulsion, according to some of the students here."

Greg was about to go on when Frank silently rose to his feet and held his finger to his lips. He had heard a floor board creak in the hall. With a bound he reached the door and flung it open.

An indistinct figure fled down the hall. Frank dashed out, but as he did, he tripped over an invisible obstruction and crashed to the floor!

CHAPTER IV

A Surly Student

RUSHING out of the room, Joe and Greg stumbled headlong over the prostrate form of Frank, who lay diagonally across the hallway.

"Greg, give Frank a hand!" Joe cried, seeing that his brother was only temporarily stunned. "I'll go after that snooper!" He sprinted down the passageway.

Rolling the stunned youth into a more comfortable position, Greg opened his collar. Then he ran for a glass of cold water. After a few sips, Frank felt better and tried to rise. Greg gripped his arms and assisted him into the room.

At this moment Joe reappeared. "The snooper got away!" he said bitterly. "Not a trace of him! How do you feel, Frank?"

"Okay," his brother murmured. "I tripped on something."

Joe returned to the hall and dropped to his knees.

Running his finger tips along the floor near the wall, the edge of his hand suddenly struck a length of limp wire. Pulling it taut, he discovered that it was knotted to the door hinge.

"Look at this!" he exploded, rising to his feet and holding up one end of the wire.

"What is it?" Frank asked.

Joe did not reply at once. Stepping to the far wall of the corridor, he stooped down. There was a hook half pulled out of the baseboard. Evidently the wire had been attached to it.

"The eavesdropper rigged this up to ensure his getaway," Joe reported.

"Boy, it really worked!" Frank agreed, rubbing his head.

"He must have wanted to conceal his identity for some reason," Greg spoke up. "Did you get a good look at him?"

"No," Frank replied, "but just before I fell I noticed one thing. As the fellow turned the corner I saw his belt—it was wide and studded with silver knobs."

"That's a good clue," Joe observed. "We'll track down every silver-knobbed belt in the place!"

"There can't be more than twenty-five students staying here between semesters," Greg spoke up. "It'll be lunchtime in an hour and all the boys will be in the dining room. We can look them over as they come in."

"Of course it's possible someone sneaked in here

from the outside," Joe remarked, "but at least we can quiz the students."

While waiting for the luncheon bell to summon them, Frank said he would like to familiarize himself with the layout of the school. This information might be useful to the Hardys in their sleuthing.

"I'll show you around," Greg offered. "I know every inch of this place well from being a student here myself."

Before starting the tour, he notified Mrs. Teevan, the cook, that the Hardys would be his luncheon guests. Then he asked the boys to follow him.

"The left wing of the building contains only bedrooms," he stated. "To the right of the center section are the offices, classrooms, labs, and dining hall."

One end of the second-floor corridor opened into a large attractive library and study hall with windows along the north and south walls. Shelves and portable stacks containing all kinds of books lent an air of dignity to the room.

As the group returned up the hallway, Greg paused before a locked door. "This was Grandfather's study," he announced. "I'm sorry I haven't a key to it with me."

"This is over the center of the dining hall," Frank remarked.

"That's right. You're certainly observant," Greg said admiringly.

The tour was interrupted by the sound of a bell outside. Greg explained that the bell was in a cupola tower on top of the building and was rung to summon students to chapel service, meals, and fire drills.

"Lunch is ready," he said.

Singly and in pairs, the holdover students of Woodson Academy straggled into the dining hall under the watchful eyes of the Hardys and Greg.

"Holy crow!" Greg said when about half of the expected diners had entered. "See what's coming!"

Two sturdily built boys approached the door, their jackets open. Both were wearing silver-studded belts! Frank drew them aside.

"Would you fellows mind waiting a second?" Frank requested in a low voice.

He and Greg accompanied them into the outer hall while Joe maintained a vigil at the door. Frank asked the surprised students where they had been during the preceding two hours. Straightforwardly they reported that they had been skating together on the river.

Judging by their expressions, Frank felt certain they were telling the truth, and said nothing about the belts. He thanked them, nodded to Greg, and the group returned to the dining room.

"No one else, so far," Joe reported. "Oh, oh, here comes one, though, and look who he is."

"Benny Tass!" Frank murmured.

To Greg, the name meant nothing. To the Hardys, however, Tass was a familiar Bayport resident. A senior at the Academy, he spent a great deal of his free time in town with a group of older boys and fancied himself to be a big shot. In contrast to this he had a reputation for bullying smaller boys both at school and in town.

When Benny spotted the Hardys he flushed unaccountably and murmured an indistinct greeting.

Frank spoke up. "Benny, that's a good-looking belt you're wearing."

"Yeah," the other answered.

"Do the studs go all the way around?" Joe asked, flipping up Tass's coat.

"Hey, cut that out!" Benny blustered. "If you like it so much, why don't you buy one?"

At this remark Joe stepped in front of the boy, blocking him.

"We were interested in the belt," he said, looking Benny straight in the eye, "because it looks just like one worn by somebody who was listening outside a certain door."

Benny fidgeted uneasily, then growled, "What door? And say, who's this guy?" He nodded toward Greg.

Frank went through the formality of an introduction and added that Greg was using the school's guest room. Tass ignored Greg's outstretched hand and turned on the Hardys.

"Are you accusing me of listening outside his door?" he asked bitingly.

Frank did not answer. Instead he said, "I'm trying to locate the person who strung a wire across the hall and tripped me."

Tass tried to hide a smirk of delight at this news but was not entirely successful.

"That's too bad," he sneered.

"Would you mind telling us," Joe interrupted, "what you've been doing for the past two hours and where you've been?"

"Why, I was—uh, ah—it's none of your business! What right have you to start checking up on me?"

"You mean you can't tell us?" Frank exclaimed.

"I mean I won't! But I wasn't anywhere near this guy's room!"

With that, Tass elbowed past the trio and moved into the dining hall. Because everyone seemed to have arrived, Greg and the Hardys selected a table near the door and were soon enjoying a satisfying lunch. When they had finished, Greg asked what the Hardys would like to do next.

"Shadow Benny Tass," Joe spoke up. "I'm not satisfied that he wasn't the snooper."

"The job's yours," said Frank. "I want to keep tabs on Henry Kurt and also learn some more about this campus."

To Joe's disappointment, Benny spent most of the afternoon alone in his room. The only time he left it was to go to Kurt's office. The bits of conversation Joe could hear through the closed door concerned a request of the student to drop his chemistry course for the second semester.

Frank learned nothing of importance either, but did get the layout of the school buildings clear in his mind—the field house and gymnasium, the riding stables, even the watchman's shed.

Just before six o'clock the brothers started for home. A mile from the Academy, on the bumpy snow-covered road, Frank became aware of another car speeding up behind him. Evidently the driver was in a great hurry, for he blasted his horn continuously.

"All right, all right, take it easy," Frank murmured, pulling as far to the right as he dared without going into a ditch. "Wait till I find a place wide enough for you to get by."

But the other driver apparently was too impatient for that. Roaring up, he started to pass with barely an inch of clearance. A split second later he sideswiped Frank and there came the sound of ripping metal. The other car skidded slightly, righted itself, and raced off.

The Hardy convertible, out of control for a moment, skidded along a few feet, then Frank brought it to a stop. Swinging the door open, he slid out to examine the damage. Joe followed. Angrily they stared at the twisted, crushed left fender.

"The idiot!" Joe cried. "That driver might have killed us!"

"And did you get a look at his passenger?" Frank exclaimed.

"No. Why?"

"He sure looked like Henry Kurt!" Frank replied.

"Good night!"

"By the way," Frank continued, pulling with all his might to get the fender away from the wheel, "did you get that car's license number?"

"No," Joe replied. "I kept watching where we were going to end up."

"Same way with me," his brother said ruefully. "Maybe there's another clue. I'm going to find that guy and make him pay for the damage!"

"Look at this!" interrupted Joe, bending down in the glare of the headlights.

Clearly outlined in the hard-packed snow were the tracks of the speeding car. One of them indicated that the left rear snow tire had a deep cut in it.

"This is a good clue," Joe stated.

"You're right," Frank agreed, as he pulled a pad and pencil from his pocket and made a sketch of the evidence. "I'll check this with Kurt's tires."

The boys drove the rest of the way home without incident. Upon arriving, they found a telephone message from Chet stating that he expected them to meet him at Biff Hooper's camp up the river late in the morning.

"We can't let him down again," Frank told his brother.

"We'll be there," Joe agreed.

Early the next day the boys took their car to a garage to be repaired. Then they set off to do several errands for their mother. The boys were walking briskly out of a hardware store when a girl's lilting voice brought them up short.

"Frank and Joe! It seems like ages since we last saw you!"

Spinning around, the brothers faced two attractive girls.

Frank smiled at the one who had called to them. "Hello, Callie!"

"Hi, Iola!" Joe said, grinning.

Callie Shaw and Iola Morton, Chet's sister, were classmates of the Hardys at Bayport High. Iola, who had shoulder-length dark hair, a tilted nose, and twinkling eyes, was a stanch rooter for Joe, who dated her for school dances. Callie, blond and vivacious, always accompanied Frank.

"You boys look as if you were on the trail of international spies—or something equally as dangerous!" Callie teased.

"You're right about the danger," Joe replied, laughing. "As a matter of fact, we're headed for the river to take a ride on Chet's new propeller sled."

"Oh, that awful thing!" Iola exclaimed. "Better make that brother of mine be careful or you'll end up in the hospital."

"We have another reason for wanting all three of you to stay in one piece," Callie added with a smile at Frank. "You're invited to take us on a sleigh hayride next week."

"That's right." Iola nodded. "It's going to be loads of fun."

Frank winked at his brother. "Okay, girls. If we survive this afternoon's ride we'll take both of you."

The boys said good-by to the girls and headed home. After a quick lunch they borrowed their father's car and rode to the Hooper camp. Rangy Biff Hooper, who had joined Chet, greeted them enthusiastically when they arrived.

"See what this character's done now," he said. "Chet's put skis on his propeller sled and wants to take us for a ride in the woods."

"Sure, it's all set," Chet told them as he revved up the repaired motor. "Hop on!"

The sled worked to perfection. Traveling along an old trail that curved and wound among the trees, it moved over the rolling countryside in an effortless glide. As they slowed to turn onto a side road, Chet burst into a Bayport High song. At the same instant, Joe gripped Frank's arm and pointed.

"Look! Those tire tracks ahead!"

Stretching out before them, and freshly made, were the telltale marks of an automobile. Every few feet along one track was the indication that one of the tires had a deep cut in it!

Joe signaled Chet to stop and they all got off the sled, while Frank told the story of the wild driver the evening before.

"The same track as the one—" Frank began when Joe interrupted.

"Yes, and there's the car, parked up ahead!"

"And look who's beside it," Biff cried in amazement. "Benny Tass—with a rifle in his hands!"

CHAPTER V

Unwanted Detectives

"WHEW, I'm glad Benny isn't pointing that gun at us!" Chet exclaimed.

The boys' surprise at seeing him with a rifle was nothing compared to the look of amazement on the face of Benny Tass when he saw them hurrying toward him. Hastily he tried to conceal the rifle, sliding it through a rear window into the back seat of the car.

"Well, Ben," Frank greeted him, "this is very interesting. Why are you carrying a gun?"

"What's that to you?" the bully snapped.

"It just happens that this property is posted against hunting!" Joe told him. "Look at all the signs around here."

"So you've been poaching, eh?" Chet prodded him.

"Oh, get out and leave me alone!" Benny cried. "This land belongs to the Academy."

"Yes, it does," Joe said. "That's why you have no right to be hunting here."

"Don't I, though? I got permission!"

The boys were startled. "From whom?" Frank wanted to know.

"Mr. Kurt!" Benny shot back. "He told me a couple of weeks ago I could hunt any time I felt like it. And he's temporary headmaster—so I guess his word's good enough!"

Lacking proof to refute Benny's claim, Joe tried a new tack. "This your car, Benny?"

"Yes, it's my car. So what?"

"Plenty. I think it's the one that hit our car last evening and almost knocked us into a ditch!" Frank exclaimed, his eyes blazing.

"You're crazy! It wasn't me!" Benny shouted, clenching his fists. "Besides, if it was at night, how could you identify the car?"

Joe pulled out the pad and compared his sketch with the imprint from the left rear tire of Benny's automobile.

"Your car has the same cut tire that the other one had!" he challenged.

Benny was purple with rage. "I wasn't even out in my car last night," he screamed.

"Didn't you ever notice that cut in your tire?" Joe pressed the attack, pointing to a deep gouge crossing the outside half of the tread.

"Sure, it's been there a couple of weeks," Benny blustered. "Maybe somebody else has a cut tire too.

You guys make me sick. I'm getting out of here."

"Not so fast," Frank told him.

He looked carefully at both bumpers. It must have been one of them which had crumpled the convertible's fender. But there seemed to be no new scratches on either of them. Was Frank wrong in his assumption, or had Benny polished the chrome surface so the evidence was gone?

As Frank paused, Benny jumped into his car and slammed the door. The motor roared, the wheels spun on the snowy ground, and the youth veered off among the trees.

"We may as well head back ourselves," Joe proposed, disappointed.

As the propeller sled skimmed over the snow with its four passengers, Frank said, "Even if we couldn't prove it, I'm sure that was Benny's car we saw last night. If Kurt was with him, and Kurt really gave Benny permission to carry a gun, I'd say the two are buddies. Funny combination."

"And worth keeping an eye on," Joe added.

Back at the Hoopers' camp, the quartet broke up. Chet and Biff headed for town. The Hardys returned to their car and drove toward Woodson Academy.

"There's Skinny Mason!" Joe called out as they went up the long drive to the school. "Let's stop and talk to him."

The boy, reporting that he had suffered no ill effects from his icy bath in the river, was so grateful to his rescuers that he embarrassed them with his thanks.

"That's all right, Skinny," Joe told him at last. "Maybe someday you can help us out."

"Gee, I hope so," the boy answered.

"Perhaps you can give us some information right now," Frank suggested.

"I'll try."

"Do any of the students here at the Academy have hunting privileges?"

"Only one that I know of," Skinny answered promptly. "Benny Tass."

"He really had permission then." Joe gazed thoughtfully at his brother. "But why is he the only one, Skinny?"

"Oh, he's Mr. Kurt's pet," the boy replied matter-of-factly. "Everybody in school knows that. Mr. Kurt even gave him a scholarship to come here so he could play basketball on our team."

"An athletic scholarship? I thought Woodson didn't give scholarships for anything but good grades!" Frank exclaimed.

"It's the only one," Skinny told him. "I don't think anybody had one before Benny. And the funny thing is that he is only about the third best player on the team."

Frank and Joe were puzzled. Why should Kurt have made such an outright exception to regular school policy?

It occurred to Frank that Skinny might become

an ally in helping them solve the mystery of the Yellow Feather.

"Did you ever hear of a guy who called himself the Yellow Feather?" he asked.

"No," Skinny replied. "What is he—a fighter?"

The Hardys laughed. "We don't know whether he is or not, but we'd like to find him. If you hear anything about him, let us know."

"I sure will," Skinny promised. "Anything else you want to know?"

As Frank pondered, Joe remarked, "Skinny, ever since Greg Woodson showed up here with a strange letter from his grandfather, this mystery about the Yellow Feather has become more and more of a puzzle."

Skinny Mason's eyes popped. "You wouldn't be talking about a letter that old Mr. Elias Woodson wrote to young Mr. Woodson, would you?" he asked.

Informed that it was, the boy hopped up and down excitedly. "I thought so! I've been wondering about that letter ever since I mailed it."

"You?" Joe exclaimed.

"Tell us more about it!" Frank urged.

"Well, the day old Mr. Woodson died," Skinny related, "I walked past the library and I saw an envelope on the ground."

"Go on," Joe said.

"So I picked it up. The envelope was all addressed and stamped and ready to mail. I could see that it was in old Mr. Woodson's writing—he had a funny little shaky handwriting. I meant to mail the letter right away, but I forgot."

"When did you mail it?" Frank asked.

Skinny paused to reflect.

"Oh, right after that they told us we'd have three days off from classes because of the headmaster's death, and most of us went home. I got all the way to Pleasantville before I noticed the letter was still in my pocket. Then I dropped it off at the post office."

"Greg did mention that the address looked washed out," Joe recalled. "It must have been caused by lying in the snow. But I wonder how it got there."

"I think I can figure that part out," Frank offered.

Before he could explain, Skinny said he must leave because he had an appointment with his chemistry teacher. The Hardys thanked him for his help and said they would see him again soon. After the boy had gone, Frank continued:

"Mr. Woodson must have been working on the cutout paper in the library and just finished addressing it when he was interrupted by someone. Apparently he didn't want this person to see the letter, so he dropped it out the window, meaning to retrieve it as soon as he could."

Joe nodded. "Only the next morning he was so ill he never had a chance to get the letter and died shortly afterward."

"I wonder if Henry Kurt might have been the

one who walked in on him," Frank mused. "Perhaps we can find out. Let's go!"

The brothers headed for the man's office. As Frank was about to rap on Kurt's door, he stopped suddenly. Somebody inside was talking excitedly.

"Those Hardys ought to be kept away from here!" shouted a rough, angry voice. It was Benny Tass's.

"They're a couple of snoopers, all right," Kurt agreed in lower tones. "So is that smart aleck of a grandson."

"Well, you ought to get 'em all out of here, somehow," Benny told him. "They're going to make trouble."

Joe stared at Frank, a quizzical smile playing around his lips at the thought of Kurt and Benny worrying over their detective work. But what now? Should they try to talk to Kurt or postpone the interview?

The boys' decision was made for them when they heard someone call, *"H-s-s-st! Frank! Joe!"*

Skinny Mason had come up behind them, and was impatiently signaling them away from the office door.

"Greg Woodson's awful sick," he whispered. "He wants you right away. He—he thinks maybe he's been poisoned!"

Following Skinny, the brothers rushed off to aid Greg. They found him lying on one of the twin beds in the guest room, writhing in pain.

"It's my stomach!" he said weakly.

"Skinny, go get the school nurse," Frank ordered.

As the boy hurried off, Greg said, "I feel better now. I got only a speck of the poison, I guess."

"How?" Joe asked.

Greg pointed to a tray on his desk. It contained a small plate on which was an untouched sandwich and a saucer bearing a nearly full cup of coffee.

"You drank some of this?" Frank queried.

"Yes. It smelled so good I took a gulp." Greg nodded. "Then I saw what was under the cup—too late."

Frank, curious, reached over and raised the cup of coffee. Underneath, lying in the middle of the saucer, was a small yellow feather!

The Yellow Feather Mystery

CHAPTER VI

An Odd Bookmark

SEEING the yellow feather and the poisoned cup of coffee, Frank set his jaw grimly.

"Greg, you're in real danger. This Yellow Feather guy means business." Suddenly Frank paused, then asked, "Where did this tray come from?"

"Why, now that you ask me, I don't know. It was on the desk when I walked in."

"This is a school tray," Frank remarked, seeing the engraved Woodson monogram. "And the dishes, too."

There was silence for several seconds while the boys pondered this new development. Joe was about to express an opinion when Skinny dashed in to say that the school nurse was on vacation.

"I'm feeling much better," Greg said. "We'll forget about nurses and doctors. Thanks, Skinny."

When the boy left, Joe said, "Before we do any-

43

thing else, I think we ought to find out what's in this coffee. Can we get into the chem lab, Greg?"

"Sure. The instructor has a key. I'll get it."

"Better not tell him what's up until we find out about the coffee," Frank advised.

"Okay. I'm a chem major," Greg said. "We'll make the test secretly."

He went for the key and led the Hardys upstairs to the laboratory. It did not take him long to find out that the doctored coffee was no prank.

"It was the Yellow Feather all right," Greg said.

"But why is he so determined to get you out of the way?" Frank wondered.

"Don't forget, this fiend has threatened Kurt, too," Joe reminded the others.

"It can't be just because of this school," Frank said. "Even with a good headmaster Woodson couldn't be a big money-maker. I believe there's a lot more to this mystery than any of us knows."

Greg was thoughtful. "Do you suppose some treasure's buried here?" he asked.

"It's anybody's guess," Frank replied. "But one thing I'm sure of. You shouldn't stay at the Academy. Your life's in danger."

"Why not go back to Myles and leave us here to take care of things?" Joe proposed.

"You're probably right. I was going today, anyway," Greg told them. "Classes start tomorrow."

The boys returned to his room, where he packed his bag. Then the Hardys accompanied Greg to his car. With a promise to keep him posted, the brothers waved him out of sight.

"What say we interview Mrs. Teevan and see if we can find out anything about that tray?" Frank proposed.

"Good idea," Joe replied.

The Academy's cook, a stout, elderly lady with white hair, was washing dishes when the boys entered the kitchen. They introduced themselves as friends of Greg's. It was obvious that the name Hardy meant nothing to her.

"We just came to ask about a tray that was sent to the guest room," Frank said.

"Oh, that," Mrs. Teevan answered. "Well, I'm not saying it was particularly thoughtful of me. You see, when I got that note—"

"What note?" Frank interrupted.

"Why, the one on the sink that told me to send a sandwich and coffee to Mr. Greg's room," she explained. "It was here when I came in from my last checkup in the dining room."

"Who left it?" Joe asked.

Mrs. Teevan shrugged. "That I don't know," she answered. "It wasn't signed."

"Have you the note?" Frank questioned.

"No. I put it in the incinerator a few minutes ago. It was printed like somebody was in a hurry and I didn't see any use in keeping it."

"There probably wasn't," Frank mused. "After you read the note, what did you do?"

"I prepared the tray and my helper—a young girl who comes in for part-time work—carried it to the guest room. She said nobody was there so she left the tray on the desk."

"Did you put a little yellow feather under the coffee cup?" Joe shot the question at her.

Mrs. Teevan looked so puzzled the boys knew that she was innocent, and explained about Greg's sudden illness and the discovery of the tiny yellow feather beneath the cup of poisoned coffee.

The woman was aghast. "Surely you don't think I would try to poison anyone, least of all Mr. Greg," she stammered in fright. "Why, my goodness—"

Overcome, Mrs. Teevan sank into a chair. The brothers hastily assured her that she was not suspected of any wrongdoing, but by now the woman was very upset.

"Yellow feather! A yellow feather! Where did I hear that before?" she repeated over and over again. "Was it old Mr. Woodson who mentioned it? I wonder—"

Frank and Joe, amazed to hear her statement, urged Mrs. Teevan to try to remember the connection with the words *yellow feather.*

"I can't seem to," the woman replied finally. "Why don't you talk to my husband?" she suggested in a quavering voice. "He's custodian of the grounds. Right now he's at our cottage resting."

Eager to follow any lead that might turn up the person who had slipped into Greg's room and tried to poison him, the boys said they would question Mr. Teevan at once. First, though, they spoke to the cook's helper. The girl denied any knowledge of what had happened to the coffee after she had put the tray on the desk.

Frank and Joe left the kitchen and hurried to the caretaker's cottage. Mr. Teevan met them at the door in his slippers and a faded lounging robe.

"Hello, boys," he greeted them affably. "I don't believe I know you. But come in."

The brothers told him who they were and followed him inside.

"I've been relaxing with a mystery story," Mr. Teevan remarked as he invited the boys to sit down. "Let's see—I'll just mark this page so I'll know where I am. Then we . . ."

"Wait! I mean, pardon me," Joe corrected his impulsive exclamation. "May I see that marker, please?"

Mr. Teevan passed the book to him. Joe opened it at the point where the man's reading had been interrupted. Grimly he showed the marker to his brother.

It was a small yellow feather!

"What's wrong?" the old man asked as he watched their tense faces.

"This bookmark!" Frank burst out. "How do you happen to be using a yellow feather, Mr. Teevan?"

"Oh, that—why, we had a pet canary," the caretaker explained. "The bird died over a year ago, and after I buried it I found one little feather near its cage. I kept it for sentimental reasons."

The elderly caretaker's explanation had such a ring of truth and sincerity that the Hardys accepted it without question. They mentioned that Mrs. Teevan had suggested their coming to see him, and gravely repeated the series of incidents that had culminated in Greg Woodson's sudden attack together with his discovery of a yellow feather under the coffee cup.

As the implications of the case sank in, Mr. Teevan paled visibly. "But Martha and I wouldn't have anything to do with—" he protested. "Why, my wife and I have been here at the Academy for more than ten years."

"We're simply trying to track down every clue we can to the identity of the Yellow Feather," Frank told him quietly. "Can you help us at all?"

When the elderly man failed to speak, Joe prompted him. "Have you ever heard anything that might help us? Your wife seemed to remember some connection with a yellow feather and old Mr. Woodson. Does that sound familiar to you?"

The caretaker, pale with worry, sank into a chair. He pressed his hand to his forehead.

"I don't know," he muttered. "It does seem familiar, but—let me think."

For several moments the elderly man remained motionless and silent while the boys waited impatiently. Then he raised his head.

"Yes, I remember now. It was about a month before Mr. Elias Woodson passed away. He came here to leave an order for me to get in town and happened to see my little feather bookmark lying on the table."

"Yes?" Joe asked tersely.

"Mr. Woodson picked up the feather and examined it for a moment, then gave me a very strange look," Mr. Teevan went on. "He mumbled something about a yellow feather getting people into trouble. I didn't understand what he meant."

"He never explained?" Frank prompted.

"No. He was getting pretty feeble. I thought it was just a case of his mind wandering, so I didn't press him for an explanation."

Frank was about to ask for more details when the door of the cottage opened and Mrs. Teevan walked into the room. Weakly, she groped for a chair.

"Martha, what's wrong?" her husband cried, helping the tottering woman to a seat.

"I'm so upset about this yellow feather business that I feel sick," she wailed. "I couldn't stay in that kitchen another minute. The girl will have to get supper alone tonight."

"I'm very sorry we disturbed you," Frank tried to apologize. "Please forget the whole thing."

"Forget!" she sobbed. "To think I was almost implicated in nearly causing Mr. Greg's death!"

"But everything turned out all right," Joe assured her.

"Yes, thank goodness. But I'm going to be accused," Mrs. Teevan sobbed. "I fixed that coffee and it had poison in it!"

The Hardys' concern for her welfare mounted as they realized the woman was close to hysteria.

"We'd better call a doctor," Frank advised, and moved across the room to the telephone.

"I'll stay here until he arrives," Joe offered. "Frank, you go back to the Academy and see what else you can find out."

"All right. Meet me near the gym in an hour," the older brother agreed.

Frank left the cottage and headed for the main building. He took a little-used trail and was deep in thought when he gave a sudden start. The young sleuth had heard the rustle of winter-dry branches in a large cluster of rhododendron which he had just passed.

He turned quickly but was too late. His arms were pinned to his sides and he was dragged from the path, struggling helplessly.

Frank glimpsed two masked faces as a gag was shoved into his mouth!

CHAPTER VII

The Masked Figure

ONE HOUR later Mrs. Teevan was resting comfortably under the doctor's care. so Joe strode up to the gymnasium to meet his brother. Seeing Skinny Mason, he called to him:

"Have you seen Frank?"

"No. But there's a pickup hockey game on the pond. Maybe he went over there. I'll show you where it is."

"I doubt it," Joe thought.

Where could his brother have gone? And what was he doing? Joe hoped he was not in trouble.

"Well, I'll take a look on the pond, anyway," Joe decided after fifteen minutes had gone by. "Lead the way, Skinny."

He led Joe to a ravine in which a frozen pond afforded a fine ice rink. There was no sign of Frank among the onlookers at the hockey game.

"Say, Skinny, maybe we'd better start searching in earnest," Joe murmured apprehensively.

Worried that perhaps the Yellow Feather had caught up with Frank, Joe led the way back to the Teevans'. He had no intention of disturbing the elderly couple; he was merely using the cottage as a starting point for a new search.

"Frank intended to go straight toward the main building from here," Joe told Skinny. "That would mean he took this path."

With his young assistant, Joe walked slowly along through the brushed flagstone path, trying to pick out his brother's footprints in the few patches of snow that were left. Suddenly Skinny stopped at a large planting of rhododendron.

"Say, look at this," he cried, pointing.

All around the bushes, marking the otherwise un-disturbed expanse of snow, were clusters of foot-prints.

"It looks to me as if there'd been a real struggle here," Joe told the wide-eyed Skinny. "And I'm sure Frank was involved in it."

"I'll look behind those bushes," Skinny offered.

"Wait! I'd better go first," Joe ordered.

He had hardly pushed the bushes aside and started down an incline when he uttered a cry and raced ahead. Half-hidden by more shrubs, a trussed figure lay twisting and squirming in a snowbank below.

"It's Frank!" he shouted.

It was the work of only a moment for Joe to whip

out a pocketknife and slash his brother's bonds. Then, while Skinny looked on in wonder, Joe cut through the gag that had prevented Frank from calling for help.

Stiff from cold, Frank could hardly move or speak. But an energetic massage by Joe revived his circulation. Then Frank told how the two masked figures had caught him by surprise.

"Did you get a look at them?" Joe asked.

"No, they had their faces pretty well covered with handkerchiefs, and wore their hats down low in front. But it wouldn't surprise me," he continued, "if one of them were Benny Tass!"

"What makes you think that?"

"One was exactly Benny's size and build. And he'd want to get square for our accusing him of running into us."

"Right. And now, we'd better get you home," Joe insisted.

As the boys walked through the woods, Skinny spoke up for the first time.

"Gee, Frank, you might have frozen to death," he said. "Do you really think Benny's that bad?"

The Hardys realized that in their excitement they had taken the boy into their confidence—perhaps unwisely. If he told the story around the school, it might be difficult for them to carry on their work. Joe was trying to formulate a request to Skinny to guard their secret when the boy saved him the trouble.

"You don't want me to say anything about this, do you?" he asked, a twinkle in his eyes. "But I'll watch Benny Tass if you like and let you know what I find out."

"Thanks," Joe said. "You're appointed!"

Skinny's chest swelled with pride. As they reached the campus, he announced that he was going to start work at once and left them.

"Before we go home, Joe," said Frank, "I think we ought to tell Kurt about the coffee incident. He may fall into a similar trap. We should warn him."

"Okay. I'll do it. You get in the car and turn on the heater," Joe proposed.

He hurried off to the headmaster's office but the man was not there. After asking a student where Kurt's bedroom was, Joe went to it and knocked.

"Yes?" a voice said. "One moment."

It was nearly a minute before the door was opened and then only part way. Kurt poked his head out. His manner was anything but cordial.

"Oh!" was all he said.

"May I come in?" Joe requested. "I have something very private to talk to you about."

"Private?" Kurt repeated. He looked more annoyed than curious. "Well, all right, come in. But I'm very busy. I can't give you but a minute."

"It won't take that long to save your life," Joe retorted, annoyed by the man's attitude.

"What do you mean?" Kurt flared.

Without wasting words Joe told the story of the poisoned coffee, suggesting that the headmaster be wary of a similar incident. To the boy's amazement, Kurt broke into a sardonic laugh.

"Well, if I ever heard a ridiculous story, that's it!" he exclaimed. "What you detectives won't dream up to get information out of people! Tell me exactly the things you want to know and I'll try to answer."

Joe was so taken aback that he was almost speechless. Angry at the affront, he turned on his heel and started from the room.

"My story is straight," he said. "Take it or leave it. I've given you the warning."

Kurt mumbled an apology, but Joe did not remain. Hurrying to the car, he jumped in and slammed the door. As Frank started the motor, he remarked:

"What's up? You look as if an ump had called you *out* on a homer!"

"That's just about right," Joe replied, and after telling Frank of Kurt's cutting remark, added, "I guess he doesn't think much of us as detectives."

"Don't let it bother you," Frank advised. "And, by the way, we'd better not mention my little adventure to Mother or Aunt Gertrude," Frank added as he guided the car toward Bayport, "or we may not be allowed to go back to Woodson."

Mimicking the tone of their spinster aunt, Joe said, "Mercy sakes, no. We'd have to put a great big mustard plaster on your chest and tuck you right into bed!"

Frank laughed, glad that Joe's good humor was restored. Then he sobered.

"What say we go back to the Academy tonight when no one's expecting us and do some sleuthing?" he asked.

"Okay," Joe replied.

At the dinner table the brothers had trouble keeping the story of the afternoon's dangers from Mrs. Hardy and Aunt Gertrude.

"Well, did you detectives run down anything today?" the latter asked.

"Not even a chicken," Joe replied with a grin. "So we've decided on a night raid to catch one."

In spite of herself, Aunt Gertrude chuckled but quickly covered it up with a discreet cough. Surprisingly she did not protest when her nephews explained to their mother that they wanted to go right back to the Academy.

"I'll trust your judgment," Mrs. Hardy agreed with a smile. "But please be careful."

"We will," they promised.

Frank picked up their repaired convertible and two hours later the brothers set off. Joe drove and decided to park the car on a small side road near the school grounds. From there they made their way carefully so as not to be seen. Reaching the campus, they found it apparently deserted and there were few lights in the windows of the main building.

"Looks as if most of the students must be asleep," Frank observed. Then suddenly he gripped Joe's arm. "Say, that lighted room up there over the dining room—isn't that Elias Woodson's study?"

"It sure is. And that room's always locked. Somebody must have sneaked in. I'm going to take a look!" Joe announced, running from hiding. When the boys reached the bay window directly beneath the study, he added, "Give me a hand up to this roof, will you?"

Frank bent over and Joe climbed to his shoulders. From there he was able to secure a sufficient grip to haul himself onto the sloping roof below the study window. Cautiously he raised his eyes to the level of the sill.

In the dim light he could see a man in a dark overcoat and hat, his back to the window, busy examining the drawers of a desk which stood against the opposite wall. Evidently disgusted at not finding something he wanted, the man slammed them shut, one after another.

Then he turned. The man was completely masked! Joe's heart pounded with excitement. Was this the Yellow Feather?

The boy watched for several minutes as the masked figure began a thorough search of the rest of the study. The intruder left nothing to chance. He upended chairs to examine the undersides and flashed a light the length and breadth of the bottom of the table top.

"I'm going in," Joe decided, noticing that the window was unlocked.

But as he moved to raise the sash, he lost his footing on the sloping roof. It was all he could do to avoid sliding off. Unfortunately, the noise alerted the masked man. As Joe grabbed the sill, he saw the intruder make for the door and disappear.

With a warning cry to his brother, Joe swung himself to the ground. In a few whispered words he told what had happened.

Together the boys raced for the main entrance of the building, which was some distance away, hoping to catch the intruder. As they reached it Frank and Joe were halted by a sudden command.

"Stop where you are!"

The voice, coming from the doorway, had a ring of authority. The order was followed by the beam of a strong flashlight which caught them squarely. Henry Kurt, bareheaded, stepped toward the Hardys, scowling.

"Oh, it's you two again!" he exclaimed, clicking off his light. "I thought you were students breaking rules. What are you doing, anyway?"

"Mr. Kurt!" Joe cried. "We just saw a masked man in Mr. Woodson's study. Help us catch him!"

The headmaster stared at them, disbelief in his eyes. "Nonsense! How could you see anyone in an upstairs room with no light in it? That room is locked, anyway."

"I'm sorry. You're wrong," Joe insisted. "The fellow was masked. I must—"

As if he were placating a small child, Kurt stepped aside and let the boys in. "Go ahead and look," he said.

He followed them up the stairs. The study door was locked and no crack of light showed beneath it.

"I hope this satisfies you," Kurt remarked with exaggerated politeness. "I'm sorry I have no key or I'd let you in. And now, with this farce behind us, I have something to say to you boys. You make up fantastic stories about other people breaking into private property. But what about yourselves?"

"What do you mean?" Frank asked. "We have permission to work on the mystery of the Yellow Feather. We haven't broken into any place."

"Oh, no?" said Kurt. "You broke into my private office."

"We did no such thing!" Joe cried indignantly.

"You come with me," Kurt commanded. "I have proof that you did!"

CHAPTER VIII

An About-face

THUNDERSTRUCK at the headmaster's ridiculous charge that they had broken into his private office, the Hardys followed him downstairs.

"We haven't been near your office," Frank said firmly. "But we're perfectly willing to look at your proof, as you call it, and clear ourselves."

The man stalked ahead of them, glancing back over his shoulder from time to time to make sure both boys were following him. Reaching the office he stopped and pointed.

"First of all," he said, "here is a jimmied lock."

Inspecting the spring catch of the door, the brothers saw that the mechanism indeed had been forced.

"What makes you think we did it?" Frank asked. "After all, anyone could have broken this lock."

"Quite right," Kurt returned with a supercilious smile. "But come inside. I have positive proof to show you."

The headmaster preceded them stiffly. Partially blocking their view of the room, he turned to face them.

"I came in here tonight to go over some papers," he said icily. "First I found the door had been forced, as you have seen. When I got inside, I discovered this!"

He stepped aside. On the table behind him, in plain sight, was a man's hand-knit scarf. Woven into it were the initials *F.H.!*

"My scarf!" Frank ejaculated.

"Just as I thought," said Kurt triumphantly. "Now suppose you explain what your scarf is doing in my private office."

Embarrassed, Frank fingered the scarf, a Christmas gift from Callie Shaw. Quickly he thought back over the day's events. Then suddenly he snapped his fingers.

"Now I know!" he exclaimed, looking Kurt straight in the eyes. "This scarf was stolen from me this afternoon during a scuffle."

"Which means," Joe added, "that someone tried to frame my brother by planting the scarf in your office!"

Kurt glanced incredulously from one boy to the other, waiting to hear more.

"And if you want to know whom I suspect," Frank decided to fire both barrels, "it's Benny Tass."

The headmaster started noticeably. Then, regaining his composure, he said, "Ridiculous! I happen to know that Tass is above that sort of thing. He's one of our finest boys. He wouldn't stoop to such a trick."

Frank and Joe disdained a reply to the claim. No use arguing with Kurt who seemed determined to be unco-operative.

"Besides," Kurt went on, looking at Frank, "why would Tass want to frame you, as your brother so forcefully expressed it?"

"That's something we'd like to find out more about," Frank returned carefully. "All we know is that he seems to have gone out of his way on a couple of occasions to make things uncomfortable for us."

He explained, as briefly as possible, about the near accident in the car at night, watching the man's face carefully to see if he would show any sign that he had been with Benny. But he got no such reaction.

Then Frank spoke of the altercation in the woods. Choosing his words cautiously, he gave details of the attack on him that morning.

"Oh, bosh!" Kurt exploded. "In no case are you sure that Tass was a guilty party. And I'm convinced he wasn't. As far as the hunting is concerned, I did give him permission, because he's older and more responsible than the other boys here."

"Then have you any idea who planted my scarf in your office?" Frank asked.

"Well, since you insist that you and Joe didn't force your way in here," the headmaster replied, "there's only one answer. I hate to say it," Kurt went on in a confidential tone, "but I'm beginning to believe it might have been the Yellow Feather. He attacked you and left the scarf here to throw suspicion away from himself."

"If he was the one in old Mr. Woodson's study, he had plenty of time to get away," Joe said unhappily.

"You know," Kurt said, "it might be a good idea if you fellows were here on the premises a little more."

"What do you mean?" Frank asked, puzzled at the sudden change in Kurt's attitude.

"Well," came the studied answer, "if the Yellow Feather is going to prowl around here at night, it might be smart to have you boys on hand to track him down." Kurt smiled magnanimously.

"I agree," Frank replied. "How about our starting tonight?"

"Very good. Take the guest room Greg vacated," Kurt offered. "Then you can start your sleuthing first thing in the morning."

The boys thanked him and started off. Nearing the door they exchanged knowing glances. Not fully trusting the man, Joe left the door open a crack in case he should want to go back and check up on Kurt's movements.

The boys did not mention their thoughts aloud. But when they reached a pay telephone booth on one side of the corridor Frank paused and said in a loud voice:

"Joe, we'd better call Mother and tell her we're staying overnight."

He thrust a hand into his trousers pocket and pulled out a coin. While Frank dialed the Hardys' number, Joe stood outside, mulling over Kurt's sudden proposal. The more the boy thought about it, the more suspicious he became.

"I wonder if Kurt's laying some sort of trap for us?" Joe asked himself.

Walking back to the office, he could hear the headmaster moving noisily about inside. The door was still slightly ajar, affording him an excellent view of the room without being seen himself.

Kurt stood in front of a filing cabinet. Reaching into his breast pocket he drew out a bunch of small keys and inserted one into the lock of the bottom drawer of the cabinet. He wrenched the compartment open almost savagely and pulled out a folded piece of white paper.

After giving it a quick glance, the headmaster smiled, then carefully put the paper in an inside pocket of his jacket. A push of his hand clicked shut the file drawer.

As Kurt walked toward the door, Joe bounded away and dashed back to the telephone booth.

"That paper must be mighty important," he said to himself.

Frank had just hung up and was stepping from the booth when Kurt walked down the corridor and spied the boys.

"Hello! Not in your room yet?" he asked, evidently annoyed. "Calling your father by any chance?"

Frank tried to ponder the import of that query as he replied, "Dad's not home yet. I called Mother to tell her where we are."

This seemed to please Kurt, who bade the Hardys good night and walked off.

"Well, what do you make of it?" Frank whispered as they climbed the stairs.

"Either Kurt means it or he's the biggest fraud alive," Joe replied.

When they reached the guest room, Joe told his brother of Kurt's actions in the office.

"What do you think was written on that paper?" he asked.

"I'd like to bet it has something to do with the Woodson estate," Frank replied. "Kurt wouldn't be so sure he can get this school if he didn't have some kind of proof. When the proper time comes, he'll produce it."

"It would be a big help if we could get a peek at that paper," Joe remarked as he threw back the blankets and sheet on one of the twin beds and lay down. "Open that window, will you?"

"Fat chance we have of looking in Kurt's pocket," Frank replied as he pushed up the sash and peered outdoors. "Wow, it's sure cold tonight. Well, I guess we're safe from attack here." He laughed. "No roofs or trellises for anyone to climb."

"If you want to make us doubly safe, lock the door," Joe said sleepily. "Good night."

Frank snapped the lock on the door to the hall, turned off the light, and soon was sound asleep. Frank had no idea how long he and Joe had been deep in slumber when he was suddenly awakened by a thud against the wall of the building. Springing out of bed, he rushed to the open window and glanced out.

Directly beneath the sill was the top of a ladder! It trembled slightly under the weight of a shadowy figure climbing stealthily upward.

CHAPTER IX

A Thwarted Intruder

By this time Joe was awake. Seeing his brother transfixed at the window, he rushed over to him and looked out into the darkness. Silently the person on the ladder continued rung by rung toward the bedroom. It was impossible from this height to identify him. Was he the Yellow Feather?

"Let's wait till he steps in before we jump him," Frank whispered.

Both boys tensed, shivering a little as the cold wind blew against them. They pressed close to the wall at each side of the window.

Suddenly the ladder gave a peculiar twist and began to slide to one side. It scraped and banged against the brick exterior, pulling the ivy vines loose in its descent to the ground. It hit the snow with a muffled thump, and the would-be intruder was flung off into a pile of snow. Struggling to his feet, he dashed away into the night.

"What luck!" Joe exclaimed. "We almost had him! Say, what happened anyway?"

"The ladder seemed to slip," Frank answered. "It might not have been balanced properly in the snow."

"Frank, do you think that was the Yellow Feather trying to get us?" Joe asked excitedly.

"It might have been," his brother replied. Locking the window, he added, "We'd better be extra-cautious the rest of the night."

But Joe had another idea. He was already reaching for his trousers. "Come on, Frank, let's go get that second-story man."

The brothers flung on their clothes and tiptoed hurriedly downstairs. They met no one in the hall or on the stairs. Evidently nobody else had heard the ladder fall. Finding the spot where the man had fallen, the boys followed his trail of footprints for a hundred yards. But here they were lost in a maze of crisscross prints which students had made earlier in the day.

Returning to the ladder, Frank flashed his light about, hunting for clues in the snow beneath their window.

"Holy crow!" he exclaimed. "Two sets of footprints!"

"So the guy had an accomplice!" Joe remarked.

"But if that were the case," Frank said reflectively, "why did he let the ladder fall?"

"Beats me," Joe answered. "They sure were a

couple of bunglers. Amateurs playing a joke, maybe?" he wondered as the boys picked up the ladder and laid it beside the building.

"I doubt that," his brother replied. "Too risky an operation."

The rest of the night passed quietly. In the morning Frank sat on the edge of his bed, yawned, and stretched. Joe was already on his feet and half-dressed.

"Toss me my trousers, will you, Joe?" his brother requested as he looked under the bed for shoes and socks.

"Where are they?" Joe's half-attentive voice returned.

"Right over there on the chair next to— Hey!" Wide awake now, Frank leaped to his feet. "They're gone!"

A quick look around confirmed the fact that his plaid slacks had been taken from the room.

"I laid them over that chair by the door," he told Joe. "You're not pulling a gag on me, are you?"

In answer, Joe walked to the door and yanked it open. The door had been unlocked during the night!

"Jumpin' catfish!" he shouted. "Whoever stole your pants could have murdered us in our beds!"

"Could be that the prowler and the pants burglar weren't the same person," Frank surmised. "But whatever the case, how am I going to get out of here without trousers?" He laughed.

"Maybe we can borrow a pair," Joe chuckled. "I'll see what I can find out."

He had hardly stepped from the room when the noise of running feet sounded through the corridor, mixed with a roar of laughter. Two or three young boys dashed wildly past, with another in their wake.

"Skinny Mason!" Joe called. "What's all the excitement about?"

"Hey, where'd you come from?" the boy asked in amazement.

"We stayed overnight," Joe answered. "What's all the hurry?"

"Somebody's pants are hanging from the bell tower!" The youngster giggled. "And they say Mr. Kurt is about to blow his top."

With a glance of astonishment and amusement at Frank, Joe rushed from the room, down the stairs, and outside the dormitory. His eyes followed the direction in which Skinny was pointing. High above the school, on the very top of the tower, were Frank's plaid slacks fluttering in the breeze!

Suddenly a voice hissed in Joe's ear, "You're a detective. How do you account for this?"

Joe wheeled to face the headmaster. "I can't account for how the pants got up there," the chagrined Joe was forced to admit, "but I can tell you whose they are—they're my brother's!"

Kurt looked at Joe in disgust. Then he turned to one of the students standing nearby.

"I want every boy in school out here within five minutes," he ordered. "Pass the word. No breakfast for anyone until this disgraceful episode is cleared up."

Since only a limited number of pupils were on hand, it did not take long to round them up. But when Kurt demanded that the culprit step forward and own up to the prank, there was nothing but a general shuffling of feet.

"I'll get to the bottom of this!" Kurt thundered.

Telling them that such behavior reflected on the dignity of the school, he quizzed the students on what they knew about the tower itself.

"The stairs to the top were condemned and torn down long ago," he stated. "Do any of you know another way the prankster could have reached the top?"

There was an uneasy silence until Benny Tass spoke up. "Maybe someone climbed out from those third-floor windows onto the catwalk around the tower and just threw the pants to the top," he suggested. "But I don't know anything about it."

Joe, at last, broke up the gathering by going for the ladder under his window. Kurt stormed for a few more minutes as to how the school ladder had gotten there. No one answered, and Joe asked Skinny to bring him a fish pole.

Then Joe propped the ladder against the wall, and holding the pole, climbed to the catwalk of the tower. A few flicks of his wrist and he cast the fish-hook into Frank's pants. Amid cheers from the on-lookers he hauled them down.

"Whose are they?" several boys asked.

Joe escaped without answering. When he brought them into the room, Frank stared in astonishment. A rueful grin that spread over his face as his brother told the story lasted only a moment, then he began to speculate on who had taken the pants.

"Are you sure you locked our door the second time?" Joe asked him.

Frank thought a moment. "No, I'm not sure. Dumb of me. I deserve what happened."

"I'm glad it wasn't any worse," Joe remarked. "Well, what say we get some breakfast and then start our sleuthing?"

Several students had already assembled in the dining room. As Frank and Joe entered, Kurt met them, anger on his face.

"There's no breakfast," he announced. "No one's in the kitchen. That good-for-nothing cook and her helper didn't show up this morning."

"Mrs. Teevan probably is still ill," Frank reminded him as they stood alone in a corner of the hall. "The doctor may have told her to stay in bed today."

"Doctor!" Kurt exclaimed. "I didn't know anything about that. What's the matter with her?"

Frank briefly explained the circumstances that led

up to the physician's visit. Kurt expressed no sympathy but burst out:

"That leaves us in a fine mess. And that assistant —just when we need her, she quits. I found her note of resignation on the sink."

"Looks as if we'll have to get our own breakfast," Frank remarked.

"The Yellow Feather is behind all this!" Kurt stormed. "I'm sure of it. He's the one who left the note ordering that tray for Greg Woodson."

Suddenly the headmaster snapped his fingers. "Why didn't I think of it before!" he exclaimed.

The boys waited for him to go on. Leaning over, he whispered confidentially, a note of glee in his voice:

"The Yellow Feather must be nearby to make such frequent visits. I'll bet I know where his hide-out is!"

"Where?" the Hardys chorused.

"The school has a camping shack out along the river," Kurt replied. "Suppose we three can find that scoundrel!"

What a contradiction this man was! Though the brothers did not like Kurt nor feel that he was sincere, still they had to admit that he was on the alert.

"It might be a good idea to look," Frank agreed thoughtfully.

He and Joe walked into the kitchen with the intention of seeing what there was for breakfast when Skinny, who had been looking everywhere for them, came to tell them that Chet Morton was at the front door.

"Chet! Up this early!" Joe exclaimed. "Something important must have happened. Come on, Frank!"

The two boys hurried to the main entrance and looked questioningly at their chum. Quickly he explained that Mrs. Hardy had telephoned him to give a message to them. She thought it best not to call direct as the wires might be tapped.

"She said your dad was in touch with her and wanted you fellows warned that you're in danger out here!" Chet whispered.

How well the Hardys knew that! But how had their father learned this?

Quickly they brought their friend up to date on what had happened and Chet whistled softly.

"Say," Joe asked him, "how would you like to hang around and do some cooking? You might pick up some clues for us."

Chet beamed. "Just lead me to the food supply."

The brothers led the way and Joe introduced him to the headmaster.

"I've found a cook!" he announced triumphantly.

"And not a bad one either!" Chet boasted, his cheeks glowing from the brisk outdoors. "I came up here on my sled to see what the Hardys were doing, and it looks as if I'll come in handy until your regular cook gets back to work, Mr. Kurt."

Frank explained Chet's fondness for food and remarked that he had developed a pronounced flair for the culinary art. When Kurt agreed to the plan, Chet grinned and said:

"All the fellows can help."

As a chef, Chet proved his ability to organize an efficient staff. Strutting about in an apron and a tall white hat which he found, Chet divided up the work so quickly that an excellent breakfast was prepared in short order.

During the meal, Joe discussed Kurt's proposal with his brother and added, "It doesn't make sense to me that a criminal would be trying to hide in a spot which might be used by students at any time."

"The Yellow Feather probably knows that most of the boys are away," Frank pointed out.

"Oh, it's possible, all right," his brother agreed. "But just the same, I'm not putting much stock in Kurt's idea."

Joe contemplated another angle. "Kurt wouldn't be trying to get us away from the school, would he, just when he has asked us to stay?"

"Anything's possible," Frank replied. "Suppose I stay here while you and Kurt go to the shack."

Joe agreed to the proposal, so Frank, after telling Kurt he wanted to help Chet get the kitchen setup organized, said he would not join the jaunt to the cabin. The headmaster looked displeased but said that he and Joe would proceed, anyway.

"We'd better go on skis," he suggested, and arranged for Joe to borrow a pair, as well as the right size shoes.

Swinging along through the woods, they soon reached a trail which Joe recognized as the one on which the boys had met Benny Tass with his car. As he was beginning to wonder if this were a favorite haunt of the unpleasant boy, Tass suddenly appeared at the side of the trail, leaning on ski poles.

"Hello, Mr. Kurt. Hi, Joe!" Benny greeted them. "What's up?" It was the friendliest he had ever been to the Hardy boy.

"Oh, we're just going to the camp-out shack," Kurt returned. "Want to come along?"

Surprised at Kurt's invitation to Tass, when they were looking for the Yellow Feather, Joe noticed a sly smile creep over Benny's face as he joined them. Joe thought, too, that Kurt seemed a bit too pleased by the addition of the new arrival.

The thought of Mr. Hardy's warning flashed into Joe's mind. Were Kurt and Tass in cahoots? Was Joe walking into unseen danger?

CHAPTER X

Cat-and-Mouse Sleuthing

"I'M GOING to watch these two like a hawk!" Joe resolved silently.

But as they slid forward through the woods his anxiety lessened, for both Kurt and Tass seemed very friendly toward him. To Joe's amazement, the headmaster told Benny of the Yellow Feather riddle and the mysterious happenings in connection with it.

"Sure is spooky business," Benny said with a quaver. "I hope we don't find the Yellow Feather in the cabin. He sounds like a good guy to stay away from."

"It's my guess he's not there," Joe spoke up and to himself added, "Kurt wouldn't dare let one of the students run the risk of meeting such a dangerous person."

As the three trudged on, the sun, which had been feeble all morning, now was blotted out. A biting wind cut their faces.

"More snow coming," Joe remarked. "We'd better make this trip snappy."

They came to a wooded hill and herringboned to the summit. Then swiftly the skiers slalomed to the bottom.

"Take it easy, boys," Kurt warned them. "We're getting close now. See, Joe, there's the cabin up ahead."

Several hundred yards away Joe could see a solidly built little stone house which looked well cared for. Kurt explained that he and Mr. Teevan came out once in a while to make sure things were in order. Neither of them had been here recently, however. As they neared the building, conversation ceased until Kurt burst out:

"Just as I thought! Someone's been living here!"

Stopping short at his remark, the boys noticed that the snow around the cabin had been trampled down in several directions.

"Look at that stack of wood by the door," Benny pointed out. "It wasn't there the last time I was out. A fellow generally has to scrounge around and get his own firewood. And he never leaves any."

"You're right," Kurt agreed. "Let's surround the place. I'll move in from this side. You two circle and close in from the front and back."

Joe agreed, since the suggestion seemed practical under the circumstances. He swung around to approach the cabin from the rear. At Kurt's signal they all advanced toward the stone shelter.

At the front door Kurt pounded and called. There was no reply.

"If anyone's here, speak up!" he shouted.

Joe watched tensely in case the Yellow Feather should jump out a window. But there was not a sign of him.

"Nobody home!" Kurt called.

The boys hurried to the door and followed him inside. The cabin was vacant. A quick scanning of the interior showed everything to be in order—the table clear, the sink clean. Kurt sniffed the air several times and headed for the fireplace.

"Smells as if—" he began.

With a poker he jabbed at the embers still lying in the fireplace. Little spots of red came to life.

"I thought so," he proclaimed with a knowing air. "Someone has been here. The fire isn't quite dead yet."

Joe did not share the man's excitement. "How about Mr. Teevan?" he asked.

Kurt gave a slight start, then said, "Impossible. He—uh—was doing another job for me this morning. No, it was the Yellow Feather!"

"Look!" Benny cried.

He was standing before the fireplace, his eyes riveted to the mantel above. Bright against the gray stone lay a tiny yellow feather!

"I knew it! I was right all along!" Kurt gloated. "The crook's trade-mark! The Yellow Feather has been living here!"

Examining the feather, Joe realized it was similar to the one that had been left under Greg's coffee cup and the same kind which Mr. Teevan used for a bookmark.

"Didn't I tell you?" Kurt said excitedly. "That crook is hanging around here, living in this cabin, and disappearing whenever he thinks someone might show up."

"It sure does look like it," Benny agreed.

Joe was not paying attention. He was thinking about Mr. Teevan. This was the second time the caretaker had come under suspicion. *Was* he the Yellow Feather or was someone trying to frame him? And why?

Wandering around, Joe's keen eyes sought other signs of occupancy, or a clue to who the intruder might have been. He found nothing.

"Well, I really ought to get back to school," Kurt remarked a few minutes later. "I have a lot of work to do before the rest of the boys return from vacation. But why don't you two stay here and see if you can't catch this Yellow Feather?"

"Sounds like a swell idea," Benny was quick to agree—a little too quick, Joe thought.

It was becoming clearer to the young sleuth that this entire setup—the investigation of the cabin, the finding of the still-warm embers, the canary feather on the mantel—might be a bit too pat to be accidental.

Had the whole trip been a contrived scheme? Joe was not certain, but the idea of being left in the cabin with Benny as a companion did not appeal to him. And furthermore, he wanted to keep track of Kurt.

"No, I think we'd better go back to school together," Joe said. "I can't see much sense in splitting our forces, and anyway, it's going to snow."

"You're not afraid to stay here, are you?" Kurt asked in evident disgust.

Benny sneered. "I thought you and your brother were such brave detectives that lying in wait at a lonely cabin wouldn't scare you at all."

Joe felt his anger rising at the insult but refused to be nettled.

"Our experience in detective work," he retorted calmly, "is exactly what makes me think it would be wise to look elsewhere for the Yellow Feather."

Kurt flushed at this observation but made no comment. Suddenly Benny exclaimed, "Say, look at this, will you?"

He pointed to a section of the flooring between the hearth and a rug. Joe reached down and rapped on the wooden boards.

"Sounds hollow," he said.

Then he pushed aside the small rug and found a knothole in one width of board. Inserting a finger, he tugged it upward. A cleverly concealed trap door rose as if by magic, revealing a narrow stairway.

"You have very sharp eyes, Benny," Joe said, feeling sure that the boy already knew about the trap door. "I'd never have noticed that door. Do you know what's down there?"

"Who, me? Why should I?" came the retort as Benny looked into the dark interior.

"Let's all explore," Kurt suggested. "Here's a flashlight. Joe, you lead the way."

"It might be better if Benny went first," Joe answered blandly. He was convinced now that his companions had some evil scheme in mind or else were just making fun of him as a detective.

"What are you turning out to be, an old lady?" Benny snorted. "I don't mind—I'll even go down there alone."

Joe let him do so to the obvious surprise of Benny and Kurt. Benny borrowed Joe's flashlight and clumped boldly down the stairs. After a brief exploration he stomped back up.

"Nothing at all down there," he reported.

Looking disgusted, Kurt announced that he would have to go back to the Academy, and that as long as Joe refused to split forces, the entire group might as well depart.

They put on their skis in silence and set off, digging their poles into the snow. The raw wind howled through the bare trees and tore at the three figures. Before they had gone half a mile the sky grew dark and a driving snowstorm descended upon them.

"Say, we're going to have trouble getting through

this," Kurt remarked nervously as the snow matted in his beard. "I can't see ten feet ahead."

Benny glanced about uneasily. "It would be awful to get lost in these woods," he said.

Joe noted that for the first time their nervousness sounded genuine. Their skiing became unsteady and they started puffing from the exertion.

Before the three had traveled a hundred yards farther, a heavy branch, weighted by snow and lashed by the wind, cracked and toppled down. It landed between Joe and Benny, who jumped several feet to avoid it.

"Maybe we should go back to the cabin and wait this out!" Benny cried.

Kurt did not agree, growling impatiently that the boys should watch where they were going. The traveling became impossible on skis and they finally took them off. The snow was not only deep but coming down so thick that the group could see only a few feet ahead of them. Again a huge limb crashed down.

"Hey, I don't want to be conked!" Benny exclaimed. "And we're off the trail!"

At last the headmaster agreed that they had better return to the cabin before their foot and ski prints were entirely covered by snow.

By the time they reached the stone building, they were exhausted. Leaning their skis beside the door they carried in some of the stacked wood and soon had a comfortable blaze in the fireplace.

"This is most unfortunate, most unfortunate!" Kurt kept murmuring as he strode back and forth like a caged lion.

The snow seemed to be coming down even harder and continued to fall steadily after evening descended.

"I guess we'll have to spend the night here,' ' Kurt concluded. "But at least we're safe from the Yellow Feather. He can't get back here."

They found several cans of food and sat gloomily around the fire to eat beans and corned-beef hash.

"We may as well go to bed right away," Benny suggested when they finished. "Then we can wake up early and get back to school. Let's bar those windows, and the door, too."

Joe helped secure the cabin, then sat cross-legged in front of the fire.

"I think I'll sit up and keep this blaze going," he said, "while you sleep."

Reluctant at first, the other two agreed and settled themselves as comfortably as they could in the cabin bunks. Joe gazed thoughtfully into the leaping firelight. He tried to sift the jumble of events that seemed to tie in with the appearance of yellow canary feathers and the disappearance of old Elias Woodson's strange cutout message to Greg.

After some time Joe noticed that the fire was getting low. All the wood they had carried in had been used up.

"I'll get an armload from the stack outside," he

murmured to himself, and quietly unbarred and opened the door.

Stepping outside, he found that the snowstorm finally had abated. It had covered the pile of wood, however, and it took Joe some time to brush several inches of the white fluff away before he could begin to gather up a load.

Stooping over to fill his arms, the boy heard a muffled footstep behind him. As he straightened up, a blunt object connected with the back of his head.

Joe pitched forward and blacked out.

CHAPTER XI

A Worrisome Search

IN THE library of Woodson Academy, Frank and Chet were poring over a pile of books. It was late afternoon and snow was pelting against the windows.

"This place would be too obvious for old Mr. Woodson to hide anything in," Chet complained. "He'd never take a chance of some student stumbling upon it."

"I'm not so sure," Frank answered. "Sometimes the obvious is the most difficult to see."

Their examination of the school library was the final stop on a tour that had produced little in the way of clues to the mystery.

"I thought your idea of a secret room, or passage, was better," Chet said regretfully. "I've always wanted to find a hidden room!"

Frank chuckled at his friend's remark, but agreed that he too had been disappointed by their failure to find any cache. Taking advantage of Kurt's absence they had spent several hours tapping the inner walls of the building but without success.

Finally Frank, recalling Skinny's tale of finding Elias Woodson's letter to Greg below the library windows, had steered their course to that room. Having uncovered nothing, they were now about to give up for the day.

"Hmm, here's a row of yearbooks," Chet commented as they walked toward the door. "I'll bet they're full of funny old-time pictures."

As he pulled out a volume to look at it, Frank scanned the row.

"A lot of them are missing," he remarked. "Let's see—Dad's class is one of them."

He wondered if the books had been borrowed or whether the collection was incomplete. After Chet and Frank had enjoyed a few laughs over the out-of-date sports pictures, Chet said:

"Let's call it quits. I'm getting hungry. Time to go back to my duties in the kitchen."

Frank agreed but said to count him out on helping. With Kurt's continued absence he wanted to take advantage of the opportunity for further sleuthing.

"I just thought of something," he said.

"What?" Chet asked.

"I found a key in a drawer of the guest room bureau. It occurred to me that maybe Greg left it there."

"You think it might open something here at school?" Chet questioned.

Frank nodded. "Maybe old Mr. Woodson's study. That mysterious intruder might even have used it!"

As Chet started down to the kitchen, Frank went for the key and tried it in the study lock. The tumblers moved and the door opened!

Frank locked himself in and got to work. It was an interesting room with heavy, carved furniture of walnut wood and paneled walls. For half an hour Frank tapped and searched. At last he came to the same conclusion Greg Woodson had: The deceased man's secret was not to be found here.

Returning to the guest room he hid the key in another drawer under the paper lining.

"Jeepers, it's late," he said, sinking into a chair. "I wonder where Joe is." Frank glanced out the window. "Some blizzard! I hope he isn't out in it."

Frank went to the kitchen. Chet was busy at the stove, with several students running errands for him between the refrigerator, the sink, and the dining room. Among them was Skinny who rushed over to Frank.

"Say, what do you suppose happened to Joe and Mr. Kurt and Benny Tass? They're all missing!"

Frank said he thought they must have been caught in the storm and had taken shelter in some safe place.

"Maybe the camp cabin," Skinny ventured.

Frank did not tell the boy why Joe and Kurt had

gone there and wondered if Benny had joined them. As time went on and the storm abated a little Frank confessed to Chet that he was fearful that the Yellow Feather might have Joe and Mr. Kurt in his clutches

"Joe could have gone home," Chet suggested. "Why don't you phone and find out?"

"I'll do it," Frank said and hurried to the telephone booth.

Aunt Gertrude answered, and in reply to his query, she said Joe had not been there. She reported, however, that Fenton Hardy had been home for an hour but had gone out again, not telling his destination. He had requested that if his sons called to tell them the FBI had no record of anyone with the nickname Yellow Feather.

"Your father also said to tell you," Miss Hardy went on, "that he thinks the paper Mr. Kurt left with him is useless. He wants you to try hard to find the one Greg Woodson lost."

After Frank had completed the telephone call, he stood lost in thought a few minutes. Although Kurt had denied it, maybe he had found Greg's paper on the river and had made a copy of it. Had he slipped up on some detail which was apparent to Mr. Hardy?

"That paper Kurt took from the file cabinet and put in his pocket might have been the original!" Frank thought excitedly. "Fat chance I'd have of finding out, though!"

Suddenly another idea came to him. On a hunch he put in a call to Myles College. A fellow student in Greg's dormitory obligingly summoned the senior from his studies. Greg instantly asked if the Hardys had uncovered any new clues.

"Well, sort of," Frank answered. "Dad thinks the cutout paper Kurt left with him is a phony. I may know where yours is, but I can't get it. Greg, do you think you could possibly remember those series of cutouts well enough to make a duplicate?"

"You mean to get all those little holes in exactly the same arrangement? I don't know. It'll be tough, but I'll try, Frank, if you really think it's important."

"I sure do."

Frank found Chet and they talked about the case, interspersing it with remarks about Joe's absence. Their worry increased with the passing hours, but when bedtime arrived, Chet tried to reassure Frank.

"Probably Joe is on the trail of that crook," he said. "By morning he'll catch him. Just wait and see."

The two boys retired to the school guest room. Chet took Joe's empty bed and slept soundly. But Frank tossed and turned a good part of the night because of his concern over his brother. Next morning his worry came into sharp focus when Kurt, with Benny Tass behind him, strode into the dining hall.

"Good morning," they both said heartily.

"Where's my brother?" Frank asked.

Kurt looked surprised. "Joe? Isn't he here? Why, that's strange!"

After explaining that he and Benny and Joe had

stayed at the cabin overnight because of the storm, Kurt went on to say that he and Benny had been awakened early that morning by cold air blowing in through the open door of the cabin.

"Joe had disappeared," he said. "I assumed that he'd made a head start to the school. His skis were gone."

Frank leaped up from his half-finished breakfast. "I'm going out to find him!" he exclaimed. "Something has happened to Joe!"

"We'll organize a searching party," Kurt proclaimed with authority.

But Frank did not wait for this nor did Chet. Rushing from the dining hall, they almost bumped into Skinny Mason.

"Say, you know how to get out to that camp cabin," Frank cried as he halted the boy. "Get your coat and lead the way, will you?"

From other students they borrowed skis and poles, and before Kurt had even begun to gather an official searching party, Frank, Chet, and Skinny were off through the woods. Fortunately, Skinny had a keen sense of direction and guided them easily to the cabin. Winded and excited, they quickly determined that Joe had not returned to the shelter since the departure of Kurt and Benny.

"Where'd he go?" Skinny asked, wide-eyed.

"Say, look at this!" Chet called from near the wood-pile. "There must have been some kind of commotion here."

Frank's sharp eyes surveyed the scene. The newly fallen snow of the blizzard was stomped down all around the stack of firewood.

"Something was dragged away through the woods!" he exclaimed, pointing to a trail of deep footprints in the snow. "You don't suppose—come on! Chet, Skinny, hurry!"

With ski poles working furiously, the boys made their way through the clearing into the woods again, and out onto the bank of the frozen Willow River.

"Looks as if the tracks lead to that old boathouse over there," Chet puffed as he followed Frank across the snow toward a rickety, unpainted shack near the river's edge.

One narrow door, half off its hinges, marked the end of the trail. Kicking off his skis, Frank yanked the door open and strode inside, with the other boys at his heels. In the dim light he saw a hunched figure face downward, lying motionless in one corner. Frank turned the bound and gagged person over.

Joe Hardy!

With quaking heart Frank felt his brother's pulse. He was alive!

"Chet, help me bring him to!" Frank cried.

He removed the gag and with a pocketknife slashed the bonds that had held his brother motionless for so many hours. Then the two boys gave him first aid. Finally, Joe was restored to consciousness. He smiled feebly but could not speak.

"You must be half-frozen," Chet groaned in sympathy, as they carried Joe out of the boathouse. "We'll carry you back to the cabin."

"At the cabin we'll make a fire and get you warmed up," Frank added.

He and Chet half-carried, half-dragged Joe to the cabin. Skinny ran on ahead and by the time they arrived he had kindled a blaze from the embers in the fireplace. Then he investigated a closet behind a small stove.

"Here's a can of broth," he announced. "I'll warm it up."

After a serving of the hot broth in front of the blazing fire, Joe recovered from his ordeal sufficiently to tell the others of the attack upon him.

"You don't think Mr. Kurt or Benny did it?" Skinny asked, aghast.

Frank and Joe exchanged glances but did not reply.

"It must have been the Yellow Feather," Chet quavered.

"I don't know," Joe replied glumly. "I wish I'd seen him, but I didn't."

An hour later Joe declared that he was able to start back to the school.

"My skis ought to be somewhere outside," he said.

"Unless they were stolen," Chet remarked.

Skinny, taking a quick turn around the cabin, found the skis half-buried in the snow and soon the four boys were ready to start back. Gliding along slowly with Frank and Chet on either side of him,

Joe proceeded steadily. Halfway there they dispatched Skinny at a faster pace to have a hot meal prepared for Joe upon his arrival. After the boy had left, Joe said:

"I didn't want to say anything in front of Skinny, but I sure don't trust either Kurt or Benny."

"Maybe we shouldn't have sent Skinny ahead to warn them!" Frank exclaimed. "I'd like to watch their faces when you show up, Joe, and see how they take it."

"It's not too late!" Chet ejaculated. "Here's where Fatty stops Skinny in time!"

With a bellow he raced ahead to catch the young messenger!

CHAPTER XII

A Near Fight

"Skin-n-y!"

Almost at the edge of the campus, the youngster heard the cry. He stopped dead in his tracks. As he turned and stared, the boy saw the chunky figure of Chet Morton emerging from the woods. He was waving a ski pole frantically, indicating that the boy was to wait for him.

In a few seconds Chet had crossed the clearing and caught up with Skinny.

"We changed our minds," Chet panted. "We have a brand-new plan. We're going to wait for Frank and Joe right here."

Leaning against the nearest tree, Chet finally caught his breath and explained that Frank and Joe wanted to be the first ones to announce the younger brother's return. In a little while the Hardys caught up with them, and all four moved on toward the school. Frank caught a glimpse of the headmaster moving about in his office.

While Chet and Skinny continued across the campus, the Hardys entered the building. As they walked in on Kurt, the headmaster whirled to face his unexpected visitors. His face was a mirror of astonishment.

"You're back, Joe!" he exclaimed in a flustered tone. "I mean, already." After a pause he added, "Fine! Fine!"

Then he looked at Joe. "You're all right?" he asked.

"Of course he's all right," Frank said quietly. "Did you expect he wouldn't be?"

"I was rather worried," the headmaster replied. "The way he went off, I didn't know . . . Joe, I'm really glad to see that you're safe. I sent out a searching party but they couldn't find you. What happened?"

As the boy explained, the brothers watched Kurt's face, but all it showed was incredulity.

"Terrible, terrible!" Kurt exclaimed. "The Yellow Feather really means business. This case is getting completely out of hand. I really think you boys had better forget about it and let your father take over."

"Not a chance!" Joe burst out. "We're solving this mystery for Greg Woodson! And what's more we want a key to this building."

"Have it your way, then," Kurt said, and reluctantly handed Joe an extra key. "But I'll not be held responsible for the outcome."

Leaving the office, the Hardys ran into Benny Tass who also appeared surprised to see Joe. Eventually he got around to a halfhearted welcome but said by way of a warning:

"You guys must be crazy to play around with that Yellow Feather. He may be a killer!"

"We'll take that chance," Frank said as the brothers moved off.

Not far down the corridor they met Chet. After hearing the headmaster's reaction, Chet told them that the searching party Kurt had organized had been sent to hunt in every direction except the area of the cabin and the old boathouse.

"That man sure is a puzzle," Chet said. "The only thing consistent about him is his appetite. Boy, can that guy put away food!"

"Say, how much longer does he expect you to give him free service as a cook?" Frank asked.

Grinning, Chet replied that he was having a wonderful time and did not care when Mrs. Teevan returned.

"The kids say the meals are better than they've been all year," the temporary chef beamed. "But if old man Kurt should look in his nearly empty freeze locker, he'll have a stroke!"

The Hardys chuckled and went to the dining room to sample Chet's good lunch. They had just finished eating when Greg Woodson appeared in the doorway. Greeting the brothers, he explained that he had been given several days leave from college.

"I've been appointed administrator of my grandfather's estate!" he announced proudly. "The court handed down the decision yesterday."

"Has Kurt heard this yet?" Frank asked, immensely pleased at the news.

"I don't know, but here he comes."

The headmaster was heading down the corridor, his face red and his jaw set.

"Looks as if another storm's going to break," Joe whispered.

Without so much as a how-do-you-do, the headmaster broke into a torrent of complaints against the legal decision about which he had just been informed by telephone.

"You—you—" He pointed a menacing finger at Greg. "You're young, inexperienced! What do you know about business? Nothing!"

Greg was furious. "Mr. Kurt," he said, his eyes blazing, "if you weren't older and headmaster here, I'd punch you right in the nose!"

The angry, raised voices instantly drew all the students from the tables. They gathered in a circle around the two men, expecting a fight.

"Greg can lick him!" one whispered.

The remark seemed to bring Kurt to his senses. He ordered the boys back to their tables, then turned on his heel and retreated down the hall. In a flash, Benny was on the scene. He stood up and said in a loud voice:

"Everything was all right here until the Hardy boys and Chet Morton butted in. Let's get rid of them!"

A few boys cheered the speech but most of them only stared in silence. Finally Benny sat down but the Hardys knew that trouble was brewing for them.

During the next few hours, Frank and Joe were snubbed and jeered and their sleuthing efforts decried. But they were not discouraged. Telling of the attack on Joe, they informed Greg of their growing suspicion against Kurt and that he might even be trying to harm them for some reason of his own.

"We haven't been able to figure out why," Frank admitted, "but we're going to keep a closer watch on him from now on."

"And on Benny Tass," Joe added.

Frank asked Greg if he had made a copy of the cutout letter.

"Not yet, but I'll do it right now," he replied.

Seated in the guest room with them, he painstakingly penciled a series of small rectangles on a sheet of stationery. Then, with scissors, he cut holes according to his drawings.

"This is about as close as I can make it from memory," he said hopefully and held it up.

The brothers studied the sheet carefully for several minutes, then Frank said, "I believe that your grandfather designed the sheet to cover a certain page in a book. The holes will reveal words. When you read them, there'll be a message."

Greg was impressed. "But what book?" he queried.

"Well, if your grandfather was working on this secret in the school library the night before his death," Joe declared, "the book is probably there."

"Let's start a search," Greg proposed.

"How about the size of the book page?" Frank asked. "Is this sheet about the same size as the one you lost?"

Greg examined it for a few moments. "I'd say this might be a trifle larger than the other sheet."

Frank recommended that they wait until evening when no students would be in the library. Around eight o'clock, with Chet on guard at the door to warn the others of anyone's approach, Greg and the Hardys went to work. Greg chose the size volumes on which they would start, and a systematic search of the shelves began.

"I'm glad," said Joe, "that we don't have to try every book in the library—only those of this general size."

However, there were enough of these to keep the boys busy, and they fitted the cutout sheet over page after page. Half an hour later, Chet, nodding in a chair, suddenly became aware of a figure moving behind the stacks about ten feet from the spot where he sat. Instantly he was wide awake.

Leaping out of his chair, Chet dashed toward the

eavesdropper. A sudden beam of light through the stacks revealed the identity of the intruder.

"Benny Tass!" Chet cried.

With Chet after him the bully raced out the door, slamming it in Chet's face.

"Tail him, Chet!" Frank ordered. "And see where he goes!" Chet disappeared.

With Joe posted at the door, the others continued to try the improvised sheet over the pages of several books. Nothing that indicated a message turned up in the holes.

"I guess I didn't get the layout right," Greg said finally in disgust. "It looks as though we're on a wild-goose chase!"

"You can't be sure," Frank told him encouragingly. "Maybe we just haven't found the right book. We're *not* going to stop until we've gone through every book this size."

They had just started on another volume when Chet burst into the room. He was red-faced and excited. For a few moments he stood gasping before the trio.

"First Benny went to see Kurt in his office!" he finally managed to report. "Benny didn't shut the door tight. They talked for a long time. Then through the crack I saw Kurt take a sealed envelope from his pocket. Without another word he handed it to Benny, who came out. I hid so he didn't see me."

"Where's Benny now?" Frank asked.

"He just ran out the front door and jumped into his car. I heard him tell someone he was driving to Bayport."

"Let's follow him!" Frank cried to Joe.

The brothers hurried from the building and raced off in their convertible in pursuit!

CHAPTER XIII

A Mysterious Envelope

THE RED taillights of Benny Tass's car winked far ahead of Frank and Joe.

"He's headed for Bayport, all right," Frank said. "But I wonder what for?"

"Don't lose him!" Joe exclaimed.

It seemed as if Benny had wings on his car. He sped over the country road at a reckless pace, and only because Frank handled the convertible with the skill of a racing driver was he able to keep the other car in sight.

When Benny hit the downtown area and ran into a series of traffic lights, he proceeded at a more reasonable rate of speed.

"Do you think he knows we're following him?" Frank mused as he drove along about a block behind Benny.

"Doesn't act like it," Joe answered laconically. "He'd be turning corners, trying to lose us."

Benny was following the most direct route toward the center of town. He drove into the main business section, found a parking place, and hopped out of his car.

From a spot half a block away, the Hardys were lucky enough to find a parking place themselves. Stepping to the sidewalk, they watched as Benny sauntered down the street.

"He's going into the office of the *Bayport Times*," Frank noted with interest, wondering what Benny could want in the newspaper office.

"That envelope Kurt gave him must be for someone in there," Joe surmised.

Before the Hardys had time to trail Benny into the building, he reappeared, got into his car, and drove speedily away.

"Shall we follow him back?" Joe asked.

Frank shook his head. "I think it would be better to find out what he was doing in the newspaper office," he advised, and Joe, upon considering the idea, agreed.

Walking into the *Times* building, they found that the man on duty behind the reception counter was a portly old gentleman they knew from previous visits.

"Well, if it isn't the Hardy boys," he greeted them. "What are you two sleuths up to now—not come to arrest me, have you?"

"No, Mr. Brown." Frank laughed. "Not this time, anyway. Maybe we'll get around to it some other day. Right now, we're just looking for a little information."

"Oh, ho, just as I thought. You're working on a case. Well, what can I do for you?"

"Just a minute ago," Frank explained, "a heavy-set fellow came in here with an envelope. Could you tell us which department it went to?"

Mr. Brown looked a trifle sheepish. "To tell you the truth, son, I don't know who brought what in. I went to get a drink of water and when I came back there was an envelope here with two one-dollar bills under it."

"Why?" Joe asked, disappointed not to learn the purpose of Benny's call at the newspaper office.

"The envelope contained an ad. The money was to pay for it."

"What did the ad say?" Frank queried.

"Now that"—Mr. Brown chuckled—"I can't tell you. It would be against the paper's rules."

The boys took the rebuff good-naturedly but were determined not to let the matter end here. One thing sure. The contents of this envelope, if it did belong to Kurt, were not what they had thought— the cutout paper.

"Can you tell us what kind of ad it was?" Frank persisted. "Was it a *For Sale* or a *Help Wanted* or an *Apartment to Rent,* for instance?"

Mr. Brown could not help but smile at the determination of the young man before him. After a pause he replied:

"I guess it wouldn't hurt to tell you that it was a *Personal* and will be in the classified section tomorrow." Then he added, "But even if I dared let you know what it said, I couldn't, because I didn't look at the ad. It's so late I was afraid the copy wouldn't get in, so I sent it right through." He tapped a delivery chute alongside him.

Thanking Mr. Brown for the information, the Hardys left the newspaper office and returned to their car.

"At least we know where to look when we get the paper," Joe said hopefully. "Maybe it'll be a clue."

"I think I'll stop home and get the cutout sheet of paper that Kurt left with Dad," Frank remarked as he swung the car from the curb. "We can say hello to Mother and Aunt Gertrude and pick up some fresh clothes."

Joe, upon reaching home and giving his mother a bear hug and receiving the usual friendly reprimand from Aunt Gertrude, glanced at Frank with a sly grin.

"Why don't we sleep here tonight?" he suggested. "I'd sure like to have a good home-cooked breakfast!"

"That's a fine way to talk about Chet's cooking," Frank chided him with mock seriousness. Then he added meaningfully, "I think we'd better go back and keep tabs on our friends."

The reference to Kurt and Tass was enough to convince Joe.

"You're right," Joe was quick to agree.

Mrs. Hardy, however, looked at her sons, an anxious expression in her eyes.

"I wish you would stay at home," she said. "I can't help feeling concerned when you're both at the Academy. Especially since your father's call, warning of danger there. If only I could have made out the rest of the message!"

The boys smiled reassuringly at their mother, and promised that they would take no unnecessary chances. Just then Aunt Gertrude called that a snack was ready.

After they had eaten, the boys changed their clothing and stowed a few extra things in an overnight bag. As they started back to the Academy, Frank patted his jacket pocket to make sure that the folded paper of rectangular cutouts was still where he had carefully tucked it.

"It will be interesting to see how this sheet compares with the one that Greg made this afternoon," he remarked.

"We'll go crazy if we try looking through all those books in the library again," Joe groaned.

Back at the school, they found that Chet and Greg were in a double room next to theirs. Greg was getting ready for bed. Chet, head propped up on three pillows, was reading a magazine.

"What happened?" he demanded.

Briefly, the Hardys recounted the chase which had led to the newspaper office. Then Frank produced

Kurt's sheet of cutouts and checked it against the one Greg had made.

"They're certainly different," Greg observed.

He was eager to try Kurt's copy on the library books. Frank was agreeable but suggested that Joe go to bed.

"You've had a brutal day," he said.

"Guess I could use some shut-eye," Joe admitted.

Chet yawned. "How about me? Breakfast, lunch, and dinner for a pack of hungry wolves."

"Okay." Frank grinned. "I'll have breakfast in bed—sausage, cakes, plenty of syrup."

"And coffee with a yellow feather," Chet said. He turned his back on the others and pretended to be snoring.

Frank and Greg, armed with a flashlight, tiptoed down the deserted corridor carrying Kurt's copy of the cutouts. They entered the library and closed the door behind them. There was not a sound but the ticking of the old-fashioned clock on the wall. Its hands stood at midnight.

The two settled themselves at a large table. With the aid of the flashlight they re-examined many of the books they had checked earlier that evening. For more than an hour they tried to obtain a combination of words that made sense.

"I guess it's hopeless," Frank conceded finally. "I'm beginning to think that your grandfather may have given Kurt a copy of the cutout sheet but not a true one."

"You mean he didn't dare give him an exact copy because he didn't trust him?" Greg asked.

"Yes. Mr. Woodson may have felt it wise to have Kurt think he was in his favor. Who knows? Being ill and maybe at Kurt's mercy, your grandfather had no choice."

"It sounds reasonable," Greg agreed. "My grandfather was a very clever man."

"If my guess is right," said Frank, "there's no use continuing our search."

"Let's head for bed," Greg proposed, and Frank followed his companion out of the library.

Their eyes accustomed to the darkness, the boys moved silently through the wing. Just before they reached the main part of the building, Frank suddenly stopped short.

"*Sss-s-t!* Greg—wait—"

Frank was staring upward at the frosted-glass transom of one of the classrooms.

"What's up?" Greg whispered.

"I'm sure I saw a light flickering in there," Frank answered. "There it is again!"

Frank gripped the knob and flung open the door. Almost with the same motion, his other hand found the switch for the overhead light. Illumination flooded the room.

A man in a dressing gown, his back to them, stood in the middle of two rows of desks. He was holding a small flashlight and seemed frozen into immobility. But in a second he turned.

"Mr. Kurt!" Greg and Frank cried.

The man blinked and for an instant a look of terror crossed his face. Then, recognizing his discoverers, he glared at them balefully.

"Why are you wandering about at this hour?" he thundered.

"We saw a light in here," Frank explained, "and came to see who the burglar was."

"I'm just inspecting the classrooms. I do it every once in a while," Kurt explained testily, walking toward them. "You needn't trouble yourselves by snooping."

On a hunch Frank moved quickly toward the spot where Kurt had been standing. Casually he glanced down at the nearest desk.

Crudely carved into its polished surface was

REVENGE HARRIS D.

CHAPTER XIV

A Puzzling Ad

KURT, noticing that Frank had seen the strange message carved into the desk, tugged nervously at his beard.

"Vandals! Destroyers of school property!" he exclaimed.

"What do you mean?" Greg asked innocently.

"I mean that boys who do things like this Harris D are a liability to the school. It costs money to replace a desk like that. Such behavior ought to be punished severely. If I had been headmaster—"

The threat went unfinished.

"Who was Harris D?" Frank inquired.

"I don't know," Kurt snorted.

"Judging from the condition of the carving, he must have been a student here several years ago," Frank speculated.

He looked hard at Kurt to see if the man were

withholding some information, but the headmaster did not flicker an eyelid.

He urged Frank and Greg into the hall and on toward their rooms. In the morning Frank told Joe what had happened.

"There must be something very important in that classroom," his brother remarked. "What could it be?"

"It certainly had something to do with that desk," Frank answered as he pulled on his sweater. "Kurt was pretty eager to get us away from it."

"Why don't we go back there and take another look at the desk?" Joe suggested. "There may be more strange words carved in it."

"And Kurt will still be in the dining hall," Frank added.

The brothers finished dressing and hurried toward the classroom. The entire corridor was deserted. No one saw them enter. Employing caution, however, Joe remained at the door while Frank crossed to the carved desk.

"Joe!" Frank gasped hoarsely.

"What is it?" Joe asked.

"Someone has removed the carved desk top!" Frank called. "There's a brand-new top here now!"

"I'm sure Harris D is the answer," Joe asserted. "If we can find him, he might give us a clue!"

The boys decided to work on this new angle as soon as possible. But first the mysterious ad in the *Personal* column of the newspaper had to be examined. Joe returned to the guest room, while Frank hastened to the entrance of the building. There he met Mr. Teevan just arriving in a station wagon with several copies of the *Bayport Times*.

"Good morning. May I borrow one of these?" Frank asked.

"Sure. You can keep it."

"How is your wife?" the young detective asked.

"Tolerably well," the custodian answered. "She ain't got over her fright completely. But I dare say she'll be around in a day or two. Well, good-by, son."

Frank waved him away, then bounded up the stairs to the guest room. Rushing in, he spread the paper on the table and turned to the *Personal* column. Quickly he ran his finger down the advertisements, pausing now and then to reread one that Kurt possibly might have sent in. As he neared the bottom of the list, Frank gave a shout.

"What is it?" Joe asked.

At this moment Greg and Chet walked into the room.

"Listen to this in the *Personal* column," Frank said excitedly. " *'Yellow Feather: Meet 100 F.R. Pt. 2101.'* "

"Jumpin' grasshoppers!" Chet exclaimed and added, "Surely Kurt didn't put that in!"

"I suppose not," Frank answered, studying the advertisement. "Unless—"

"Unless what?" Greg asked.

"Kurt might have put it in to send us on some

wild-goose chase," Frank replied. "I'm convinced that he'd go to great lengths to get rid of us."

"In which case you won't move a step away from here," Greg said firmly.

Joe reminded the young man that this was all guesswork. Kurt might not have been responsible for the ad. Joe felt the boys should figure out the code message and go after the Yellow Feather.

"What could it mean?" Chet asked, repeating the words. "There's no doubt about the Yellow Feather part. It's a message from someone to him."

"One hundred F.R. Pt.," Frank said, "isn't very clear. One hundred what? Feet, maybe? One hundred feet R. Pt."

"Rocky Point on Barmet Bay!" Chet exclaimed. "I'll bet a cookie—a box of 'em. One hundred feet off Rocky Point."

"A meeting place," Greg agreed. "Sounds logical. Then they must have boats."

"But the rest of it," Frank said; "two thousand, one hundred and one. Twenty-one O one—don't you get it?" he asked. "The military and naval way of telling time. Twenty-one means nine P.M., and the O one means one minute after nine."

" 'Meet one hundred feet off Rocky Point at one minute past nine P.M.' " Joe read the complete message. "Wow! We've cracked their code!"

"There's only one thing for us to do, Joe. Catch them in the act."

"In our own boat, you mean," his brother said,

thinking of their sleek motorboat the *Sleuth* stored in the Hardys' private boathouse on the bay.

"No, I wasn't thinking of using the *Sleuth*," Frank corrected him. "We'd be smarter not to take our own boat—someone might be watching for us to start out in it and follow us."

"Then how about Tony Prito?" Joe suggested. "He says his *Napoli* is in good shape and I know he'll be glad to take us."

"Good idea," Frank approved. "I'll telephone him."

"Well, I'm glad you don't want me to go," Chet spoke up. "Operation Sub-zero—br-r-r!"

The Hardys looked at Greg. "I think," said Frank, "that Joe and I should do this job alone. I'd hate to have you get in a jam. Anyway, both you fellows ought to stay here and keep your eyes on things."

After breakfast, Frank called Tony Prito. The star end of Bayport High's football team and close friend of the Hardys and Chet, Tony was always ready for adventure. He assured Frank that he would be delighted to take them out.

"Meet me at eight o'clock," he told them. "Drive out the shore road, and I'll have the *Napoli* waiting for you in Segram's Cove."

Frank had just stepped from the booth when a familiar voice called:

"Hi, Frank!"

"Skinny! Say, you're just the person I need."

"Swell. What can I do for you?"

"Play detective. Find Benny Tass and ask how he got permission to go to Bayport last night. Tell him you heard that he was seen there at the newspaper office putting an ad in the paper. Report to me how he reacts and what he says."

Skinny said he would do it at once. But as he started off, another thought came to Frank and he called him back.

"Did you ever hear of an alumnus of Woodson Academy called Harris D?" he asked.

Skinny's forehead wrinkled. "Harris D—would you mean Harris Dilleau by any chance?"

"Maybe. Who was he and when was he here?"

"Why, a long time ago—I've heard my uncle John Mason talk about him several times. He was in the same class. Uncle John graduated about twenty-two years ago."

"What did he say about Dilleau, Skinny?" Frank was intensely interested.

"Oh, he was a real troublemaker, my uncle said. I think he was expelled from school."

The boys separated and Frank went to the guest room to relay this latest bit of information to Joe.

"Now we're getting somewhere!" Joe cried. "Let's go to the library and see if we can find out anything more about Dilleau in the yearbooks."

But as they scanned the row of annuals, they became discouraged. There was only one publication which dealt with Dilleau's years at Woodson. Although Skinny's uncle was mentioned prominently, there was only one short reference to Harris D.

In disgust Joe returned the volume to its proper place. "I'm going to search the library for the missing yearbooks," he declared, "and see if they contain any information about Dilleau. I'll bet he's a friend of Kurt's."

During the day he examined shelf after shelf of books in his hunt for the missing volumes, but drew a blank. Frank busied himself trailing Kurt. The headmaster's activities, however, were above suspicion.

The only worth-while information came from Skinny. Benny Tass had admitted to him that he had gone to the *Bayport Times* with an advertisement but it had not appeared in today's paper.

"He said he got there too late," Skinny concluded his report.

The Hardys, with no evidence to disprove this part of the story, had to accept it. So it was with little thought of Kurt that they set out that evening to get a line on the Yellow Feather and perhaps capture him.

They drove to the rendezvous spot by a circuitous route in order to throw off any possible followers, but reached the bay shore at exactly eight o'clock.

Frank cast the car headlights over the water, and the beams picked up Tony in his motorboat. Looking quickly across the water to fix in his mind the position of the waiting craft, Frank turned off the lights, locked the car, and the boys started down the slippery embankment.

A sudden sound of a muffled engine reached their ears and they ducked behind a pile of fishermen's equipment. The brief tension ended, however, when they heard Tony's voice as the bow of the *Napoli* scraped softly against the low dock.

An instant later Tony was ashore, running up the snowy slope to meet them.

"It's no use," he reported. "We can't go. There's too much floating ice in the bay!"

"We can't give up the trip!" Frank cried. "Why, we may never get another break like this!"

CHAPTER XV

Flying Harpoons

GIVE up a chance to capture the Yellow Feather? A groan of disappointment came from Joe.

"Tony," he said, "this might be our only hope of catching the Yellow Feather!"

The *Napoli's* skipper, his face almost hidden in his fleece-lined coat and hood, shrugged. "The whole bay is full of great chunks of ice, Joe," he said. "If we hit one of those floes, it would knock a hole in the hull so fast we'd sink like a rock."

Through the darkness, the boys could dimly see the white forms of thick ice bobbing up and down on the water. There was a constant swish and booming as the surf caused them to bump, and when the wind blew in sudden gusts, the icy mass made a creaking and groaning sound.

"Miniature icebergs," Frank observed. "I sure hate to miss this opportunity of perhaps solving the mystery, though."

"I'll tell you what," Tony spoke up. "I'm willing to risk the boat. You fellows pilot her. You're better navigators than I am."

Frank turned to his brother. "What do you think, Joe?"

"It's Tony's boat," Joe replied. "As for me, I'm game if you are."

"Then let's go!" Tony agreed.

All three sprinted out on the slippery dock and jumped into the *Napoli*.

"Take her away!" Tony urged as the engine sprang to life.

"You take the wheel, Frank," his brother said. "I'll cast off."

Joe released the line as Tony checked the fuel gauge with a small flashlight.

"Be careful you don't open her up when we get near the Point," Tony warned. "The sound will carry."

Frank assured Tony he would use care and eased the sleek craft out into the ice-jammed water. Since he did not wish to betray their presence to anybody involved in the mysterious rendezvous, he decided to proceed without lights.

"Joe, crawl onto the bow and tell me where to steer," he directed.

"Okay."

Joe felt his way forward in the dark. Lying on the deck with his head hanging over the prow, he kept up a rapid-fire series of instructions to his brother. Trimmed perfectly, the motorboat responded to Frank's lightest touch. Tony sat beside him, watching in admiration at the deft manner in which the boys handled the craft.

"Who would ever keep an appointment out here in the bay on a night like this?" Tony asked in amazement as the *Napoli* snaked slowly among the floating chunks of ice.

Frank managed a grim smile. "You mean, who besides us? I don't know, except the Yellow Feather!"

As the boat moved farther and farther out of the cove the danger from the ice increased. Instead of the profusion of the tightly packed floes, through which the boys could thread their way with little trouble, they faced now, in the open water, the menace of stray jagged sections that could smash a hole in the hull as easily as a fist through paper.

"Frank, port, hard!" Joe's terse command came like a whiplash.

Desperately, Frank spun the wheel. There was a slight scraping sound all along the starboard gunwale, and a gasp of relief from Joe as the ominous section of ice floated astern.

"That was close!" he whispered hoarsely.

"How far off Rocky Point are we, Tony?" Frank asked, peering into the darkness. "I can't see a thing."

"We must be getting close now, I'd say. Maybe you'd better cut 'er down some. You can almost drift in."

In the booming of the surf against the rocks, the muffled sound of the *Napoli's* motor was nearly lost. As the motorboat drew closer to the Point it rolled sharply in the choppy waves.

"See anything ahead there, Joe?" Frank called in a low voice.

"Not a thing. Nothing that even looks like a boat."

In a few moments they were in the shadow of the sheer rocks of the Point that towered menacingly above them. The *Napoli* was crawling now. Joe kept a constant watch for ice floes, while Tony searched the sea for the shadowy outline of another craft.

Suddenly there was the sharp *boi-i-ng* whine of a projectile over their heads! Instinctively the boys ducked. *Splash!* The object struck the water ten feet from the craft.

Frank's hand grabbed the throttle and with a roar the speedboat leaped ahead.

"Where'd that come from?" Joe called.

Neither Frank nor Tony could answer. Something had landed in the water beside them, but whether it had been sent from the shore or from another boat, there was no way of telling. It was impossible to tell the direction from which it had come.

Before the craft had gone twenty yards there was another *twang* and the same whine. This time all three felt a convulsive shudder jar the boat. The *Napoli* had been hit!

"Look at this!" Tony cried in consternation, leaning over the side.

The tip of a small harpoon was embedded in the wood of the boat about a foot above the water line. Tony wrenched the missile loose and pulled it into the cockpit.

"Holy crow!" Tony exclaimed. "Let's get out of here quick. Whoever is firing these things has got us in range!"

Frank spun hard to starboard and the *Napoli* lurched seaward. A second later there came another twang, followed by a splash of water sending a spout high into the air directly in front of them.

"We're in a trap!" Frank exclaimed. "Our only chance is to hide!"

Pulling on the wheel frantically, he headed the boat recklessly back toward the protection of the rocks.

"Frank! Ice!" Joe warned him.

Dead ahead, blocking their course to the safe shelter of the Point, was what looked like a whole flotilla of ice floes! Frank realized that it would be almost impossible to steer through them. Desperately his keen eyes pierced the darkness for an escape route. In a flash, he saw the only possible way out of their hazardous situation.

"Joe! Come back here!" he called.

At the same time he cut the throttle, spinning the

wheel first one way, then the other, so that the *Napoli's* zigzagging course made the boat a difficult target to hit.

Joe crawled back along the deck and jumped to his brother's side. Quickly Frank whispered his plan. Instantly Joe grabbed a boat hook and slid up to the bow again. At the same time Frank cupped his hands to his mouth and yelled at the top of his lungs:

"Help! We're sinking! Save us!"

In the moment of silence that followed, he steered the speedboat straight toward an overhanging cliff, and the *Napoli* was drawn under the jutting cover. With the boat hook Joe kept the craft from bouncing against the rocks.

The boys waited. No more *whangs* of death-dealing harpoons. The ruse had worked!

"Where do you suppose the harpoons were fired from?" Tony whispered as they sat tensely waiting for the enemy to make his next move.

"They seemed to come out of nowhere," Joe replied in a low voice. "I didn't even hear the sound of a gun firing them, did you?"

"No," the others answered.

"What puzzles me," Frank mused, "is that funny *twang* we heard just before the harpoons landed."

"Hold it!" Joe demanded. "Listen!"

In the crash of surf and the whistle of wind they heard another sound.

"A motorboat!" Frank said hoarsely.

Its engine muffled, the unseen craft was evidently

speeding toward them. The noise grew louder with every second.

"Do you suppose he knows we're here?" Tony asked fearfully. "If not, there's going to be a crash!"

"Let's move," Joe suggested.

"But where? We don't dare show ourselves," Frank objected. "I say, take a chance and stay here."

The mysterious boat continued to come in their direction at breakneck speed.

"That fellow must be crazy to be traveling that fast!" Frank exclaimed.

"This is it!" Joe announced tersely as the other craft did not swerve. "Get ready for a fight with the Yellow Feather!"

CHAPTER XVI

Dangerous Waters

THEY waited tensely while the sound of the approaching motor came closer. Then the outline of another speedboat took form in the darkness, zigzagging about fifty yards off their starboard side.

"It's searching for us!" Frank whispered in Joe's ear.

The craft was almost abreast of their hiding place when a waterspout seemed to rise directly in front of it.

"Another harpoon shot!" Joe exclaimed. "That boat's being fired on, too."

The pilot of the second craft seemed taken by surprise. For a second there was no reaction, then the boat practically jumped from the sea as its skipper gave it the gun. But even as he did, another big splash rose alongside the craft. It veered sharply to one side.

By this time it was evident to the Hardys that the

harpoons must be coming from the high rocks of the Point rather than from a boat.

"Whoever's in that boat doesn't have any more return fire than we do," Frank said tensely. "He's going to make a run for it!"

"Why don't we make our break now also?" Joe suggested. "With two of us out there, it would divide the target."

"Okay," Frank agreed. "Besides, I'd like to see who's in that boat."

He started the motor and the instant it caught he waved Joe to let go with his grappling hook. The *Napoli* streaked forward, angling from left to right at high speed.

"We'll be out of range in a minute!" Frank yelled. "Then we'll take off after that other boat."

The boys saw one more big splash behind them. After that no more came. The pilot of the craft ahead had opened up and ripped off in a straight course toward Bayport.

"That fellow can really handle a boat," Tony remarked, as they watched the craft cut between ice floes without losing speed or direction.

His mouth set in a grim line, Frank trailed the other craft. But in spite of the wide-open throttle and a path to follow, he could not gain on it.

"That fellow cuts through the ice field as if he had radar!" Joe marveled.

"We'd better let him go before we crack up the *Napoli!*" Frank said. "How about my taking the boat right into your boathouse, Tony, instead of Segram's Cove? That hole the harpoon made ought to be checked right away."

"You're right. I'll drive you back to the cove in my jalopy so that you can pick up your car," Tony suggested.

When they reached the boathouse, the boys used a block and tackle rigged to an electric motor and hauled the *Napoli* up on rollers to examine the damage.

"Not as bad as I thought it would be," Tony said smiling, as he looked proudly at the boat which had brought them through a near disaster.

"I'm relieved," said Frank. "Just the same it will cost something to fix. Joe and I will pay for the repairs."

Tony would not consent to this, and the Hardys could not change his mind.

"It's all in the cause of detective work," he said, grinning.

"Well, at least let us help you patch it. Got any stuff here?"

"No."

"We have some in our boathouse," Joe said.

"Okay," Tony said. "Let's go get it and I'll make the repairs tomorrow."

The three boys hurried to the Hardy boathouse, which was not far from Tony's. Frank unlocked the door and switched on the light. The trim *Sleuth* gleamed in her berth.

"Hey, she's wet!" Joe cried suddenly. He jumped in and felt the motor. "Why, she's just been used!"

The next instant Tony groaned. "There's a small hole in her side just like the one the harpoon put in the *Napoli!*"

The boys looked at one another in consternation.

"Listen, if those crooks think they can steal our own boat to chase us in—" Joe began.

Suddenly Frank burst into laughter. Tony and Joe stared at him in amazement.

"I think I know whom we were chasing," Frank chuckled. "Detective Fenton Hardy!"

"What! Your dad?" Tony gasped.

"No wonder he outmaneuvered us," Joe said, grinning. "Dad's the only one I know who handles a boat that well."

Frank laughed. "Will we give him a cross-examination!"

He quickly found the calking material and handed it to Tony.

"Thanks," Tony said. "I know you fellows want to get home, so I'll drive you to your car pronto."

A little while later he dropped them off. Joe slid behind the wheel of the convertible and drove home.

Bursting into the living room, they found their father in lounging jacket and slippers before the fireplace. He was reading an FBI report. Mr. Hardy looked up at his sons with raised eyebrows.

"What's all the excitement about?" he asked.

"And those grins," he added, noting the looks of amusement on his sons' faces.

"We were out for a ride in Tony's speedboat," Frank told him. "Nice night for a boat ride, wasn't it, Dad?"

The young detectives eagerly watched their father's face to see what his reaction would be, but he maintained a puzzled expression. Joe touched his fingers against his father's tousled hair.

"Um, damp," he said. "Couldn't be from the salt spray, could it?"

The corners of Mr. Hardy's mouth crinkled and he broke into a hearty laugh. "All right, you win!" he said. "I'll have to be more clever to throw you off my trail."

Frank grew serious. "Dad, you no doubt have some different slants about this whole case than we do. What's your theory of the reasons behind all this funny business?"

"Well, I happened to notice the ad about the Yellow Feather in today's paper," Mr. Hardy explained, "and called the school to ask if you had seen it. When Chet told me where you'd gone, I decided you might be headed for trouble."

"So you followed to protect us?" Joe asked.

"That was one reason, although I knew you could take care of yourselves. I wanted to trap the Yellow Feather!"

Frank told his father about trailing Benny to the *Times* office, and the discovery of the advertisement.

"So you figured out the code, too," Mr. Hardy remarked. "Well, it was simple, and that's what makes me think it was planted."

"You mean by the Yellow Feather?" Joe asked.

"Possibly. In any case it was designed to harm one, two, or three of us and put us off the case for good."

Frank had been mulling over other angles of the mystery and said little. But now, fitting the various pieces of the puzzle together, he asked:

"Dad, now that we know Kurt is tied up in this somewhere, do you think he could be the Yellow Feather?"

"Until I have more proof, I'll reserve judgment on that point. I do believe, though, that he's trying to steal the Woodson estate from Greg, and perhaps old Elias was afraid of him. The paper Kurt gave me is a complete phony."

"Really?" Frank said. "Was that the reason you called Mother about us being in danger at the Academy?"

"Yes," his father replied. "When I realized the cutout copy was a false one, I became convinced of Kurt's dishonesty and that he would stop at nothing to gain what he wants."

"Don't worry, Dad," Joe spoke up. "We certainly don't trust that character either. He won't catch us off guard."

"Good," said Mr. Hardy. "Of course I know you two aren't easily taken in."

"How did you find out that the cutout paper Kurt gave you is a phony?" Frank asked his father.

"I decided that the slots in it were supposed to represent words," the veteran sleuth explained. "So I had the paper reduced to card size. Then I used a calculating machine to show me every possible combination of words of the lengths indicated by the slots."

"Pretty neat!" Joe said admiringly.

"Yes, but no message was revealed that could have any bearing whatsoever on this case. That's why we must get back the original which Greg lost."

Joe told of his suspicions that Henry Kurt might have the original sheet and be keeping it locked up in his office filing cabinet.

"I saw him take a paper out and put it in his pocket," Joe went on. "Maybe when no one is around he tries to figure out what the cutouts mean."

"That's very likely," his father agreed. "I think that Kurt made the phony one he left with me as a cover-up for his own underhanded work."

"Will you give up the case?" Frank asked.

"Indeed not. But I'll proceed along different lines. Again I warn you both to watch your step. And concentrate on trying to locate the original cutout sheet."

Not wishing to be away too long from the main scene of operations, the brothers bade their family good-by and took off for the Academy. They were halfway along the winding country road when Joe noticed a peculiar reflection in the sky.

"Looks like a fire," he said excitedly. "Frank! Do you suppose—the school?"

His brother gave the car more gas and the convertible roared along the road. Frank braked to a stop at the edge of a field that bordered the campus.

Before them an immense bonfire was sending flames high into the air. In its flickering light was a group of excited students.

"Say, what is this?" Frank murmured, jumping from the car.

"There's Skinny. And Chet," Joe said, sliding out after his brother.

"And Benny," Frank added, almost bumping into the bully. "What's going on, Tass?"

"Semester celebration! We don't have to go to bed till we want to. It was Kurt's idea. Great fun. He even gave us a lot of the old record books to burn up."

"Record books! He can't do that!" Frank cried in dismay. Turning to Joe, he whispered, "If those records are destroyed, we'll never find out anything about Harris Dilleau."

The brothers ran over to Chet and took him aside.

"Where's Greg?" Joe asked. "He'd better order the boys not to burn those records!"

"Greg's gone," Chet informed them. "He received a message calling him back to college."

Realizing that there was no time to lose if he

wanted to save the records, Frank leaped between
the fire and the students.

"Fellows!" he cried. "We have to put out this fire
—and fast! Important papers are being burned by
mistake. Grab all the snow you can hold and throw
it on the flames!"

But before the students could carry out the order,
Benny jumped forward and shouted, "Bunk! Why
should we put it out just because you say so? It's
been a long time since we had a fire like this!"

"There are valuable school records in there,"
Frank retorted. "We must save them!"

Impatiently Frank leaped to a nearby snowbank
and swept up an armload of snow. But as he turned
to run and throw it on the fire, the bulky figure of
Benny Tass blocked his path.

CHAPTER XVII

A Disastrous Fire

"Look out, Frank!"

Joe's warning shout cut through the hubbub of excited students, but it came too late.

As Frank ran toward the flames he did not see Benny's foot, which the bully had stuck out deliberately to trip him. The young detective sprawled headfirst toward the fire.

"Oh!" cried several of the younger boys.

Like a cat, Joe pounced after his brother and grabbed Frank's coat. Pulling him clear of the blaze before it had time to ignite his clothing, he helped Frank to his feet.

"Is he all right?" Skinny cried, seeing Frank's blackened face.

Anxiously everyone gazed at the unfortunate boy, who rubbed his face with a heavy glove. The only apparent injury was a pair of singed eyebrows.

Frank's ski cap and turned-up collar had saved him from any bad burns.

Upon learning that Frank was all right, Chet angrily faced Benny. "That was a dirty trick," he said.

The students gathered around, sensing a fight, and there were growls of disapproval from many of them.

"It was an accident," Benny declared, as Chet doubled up his fists. "I'm sorry."

Despite Benny's apology, the onlookers stared at one another in disbelief. A few minutes previously, most of the Academy students had been ready to side with Tass. Now the entire group turned against him.

"Let's put out that fire as Frank said!" one of them shouted.

Before Benny could protest, the students began to throw snow on the flames.

"Here's a fire extinguisher," cried Skinny, who had run to the school's garage for the cylindrical container.

Between the extinguisher and the concentration of snow heaped on the giant blaze, it soon died down. Chet, meanwhile, had hurried off to the school's tool shed and soon returned with two steel rakes. Joe grabbed one. Together the boys pried into the sodden mass, yanking out what was left of the record books.

"Oh, good night!" Joe moaned in dismay. "The fire extinguisher has ruined what the fire didn't."

The pages of the book he had picked up were almost blank, except for some blurred, washed-out traces of inked writing.

"Maybe not all of them are ruined," Frank said hopefully, and the raking went on.

Several students helped, using their gloved fingers. Soon there was a mass of partly charred papers stacked up in the snow.

Off to one side, Benny Tass was still complaining bitterly. "It's a fine thing," he blustered, "when we let a couple of smart alecks from town come on the campus and tell us when we can and when we can't have a celebration!"

Most of the boys ignored him, but his few close buddies stood by him.

"Oh, ho!" exclaimed one of Tass's pals. "Here comes Mr. Kurt. Wait till he hears about this."

The headmaster stomped onto the scene and was immediately stopped by Benny, who told him how the Hardys had ordered the fire doused. Kurt stormed over to where the boys were still trying to salvage some of the records.

"What's the idea?" he barked. "I gave full permission for that bonfire. Isn't that sufficient authority? By what right did you countermand my orders?"

Frank stepped up to the headmaster. "Mr. Kurt, you know as well as I do that Gregory Woodson wouldn't want any records of this school burned," he said evenly.

"But I'm in charge here," Kurt said pompously.

"I'd like to remind you," Frank replied, "that Greg Woodson has been named by the court as administrator of his grandfather's estate. The school and its records are a valuable part of that estate."

Kurt was speechless with rage. He waved his arms and pointed a finger at the Hardys, but no words came from his lips.

Joe took up the accusation. "The destruction of the records of an estate could turn out to be a criminal offense!" he said.

Kurt finally found his voice. "Not these!" he shouted. "I'd looked over all the records. There wasn't anything valuable in them." After a slight pause he said threateningly, "You Hardys will regret this. No one can come in here and tamper with my authority!"

"No one's trying to do that," Frank said. "But we're going to save Woodson Academy for its rightful owner."

At a murmur from the students, Kurt suddenly realized that he had lost face with them. Purple with rage he stalked off, ordering his young charges to follow him. From a distance the Hardys and Chet could hear him trying to explain his side of the case and saying he was sorry to have lost his temper.

The unpleasant scene over, the boys returned to their salvage work. Soon every readable scrap had been gathered up into a small pile.

"I sure hope there's a clue to this mystery in here

to make our work worth while," Chet puffed. "Maybe Kurt was right."

"I think just the opposite might be true," Frank spoke up. "They might contain items he doesn't want us to see. If only those particular ones didn't burn or weren't ruined by the fire extinguisher."

"Here's an idea," Joe said. "Kurt probably gave the telltale ones to the boys first. They would have been on the bottom of the pile."

"And were saved!" Chet chortled, his enthusiasm returning. "Say, fellows, we ought to hide these papers so Kurt can't find them."

"Or the Yellow Feather or Tass," Joe agreed.

"We could take them to your room," said Chet, then chuckled. "But after the way Frank's trousers wound up on top of the bell tower, I wouldn't say it's a safe place."

Chet then proposed locking them in one of the kitchen cabinets, but both brothers vetoed that area as being too accessible.

"I know," said Frank at last. "Let's hide the papers in the tool shed. Unless we're spotted moving them in, no one would think of looking in there."

Frank's proposal was agreed upon. Making sure that nobody was in sight, the boys split the pile of charred records into three armloads and carried them, together with the rakes, to the shed.

By the light of a lantern which they found, the three stacked the remains of the records in a corner and covered them with a tarpaulin. The Hardys would investigate the contents in the morning. Frank had found a padlock with a key which he was about to snap on the outside of the door when Chet spoke up.

"I have a better idea," he said. "One of us really ought to stay here and stand guard over these papers. You fellows must be dead tired after all you've been through today, so I'll stay here."

Frank looked at him dubiously.

"Don't worry," Chet assured him. "You lock me in and everything will be all right." He grinned at his friends a little nervously but insisted upon remaining.

"Okay," Frank said. "You're a real pal."

With Chet inside the shed, he locked the door and departed quickly with Joe for their room.

Chet relighted the lantern and set it on a workbench. As he glanced about, shadows of rakes and shovels danced weirdly on the walls. A bit scared in the cold, eerie atmosphere, Chet did not feel like sleeping. He got to wondering how Frank and Joe would have passed the time.

That was easy. They would be looking in the pile of records for clues.

"That's what I'll do," Chet decided. "Maybe I can come up with a surprise for the fellows."

One by one, he began going through the papers. The pile of discarded possibilities was growing high when suddenly Chet's eye lighted on an interesting item.

"Boy oh boy!" he murmured.

At the same instant Chet became aware of a scraping sound outside the shed. Quickly extinguishing the lantern he peered outside. It was so dark he could not see a thing at first. But as his eyes adjusted themselves to the change, some of the blackness took shape. It seemed to be moving!

As Chet watched, terrified, the moving object became a person. Was he heading for the tool shed?

Instinctively the youth started to drop out of sight, in case a light should be flashed in his direction. Before he got below the level of the sill, there was a crash of glass and something hit him full force on the chest.

Chet sagged to the floor.

CHAPTER XVIII

A Minor Explosion

EARLY the next morning Frank and Joe hopped out of bed and dressed quickly.

"I wonder how Chet made out last night," Frank mused as he and his brother left their room and dashed downstairs.

Joe grinned as he opened the front door. "We'll probably find him lying sound asleep smack on top of the records!"

They hurried toward the tool shed, first making sure that no one was following them.

"Bet our friend Chet is ready for breakfast," Joe observed, nearing the tool house.

Suddenly both boys uttered cries of alarm. Crudely painted on the side of the shed was a large yellow feather! Fearful now that something might have happened to Chet, the Hardys raced forward. Getting closer, they saw a hole in the windowpane the size of a half dollar. A second later a bound and gagged figure rose into view behind the glass. *Chet Morton!*

The prisoner's hair was disheveled and there was a smear of blood on one cheek.

"That Yellow Feather is a fiend!" Frank exclaimed as he hastily unlocked the door and rushed inside.

He removed Chet's gag while Joe cut the bonds that held his friend's arms.

"For Pete's sake!" Frank said. "What happened? And are you all right?"

"Guess so. I was conked," Chet replied, rubbing a bruise over his left ear. "Somebody shot at me. I went out like a light. Didn't come to for hours. I just managed to get up."

"Say," said Joe, bending down to pick something off the floor, "I'll bet this is what hit you!"

In his hand was a small dart. It was about six inches long and had a leather-covered knob at one end.

"The kind that can be fired from a gun!" Frank cried excitedly. Then another thought struck him. "Chet, the records!"

"They're—they're gone," Chet said absently.

Joe leaped to the corner in which the papers had been stacked the night before and groaned. All their work for nothing!

"We really have been taken in by the Yellow Feather," Frank said sheepishly as he turned to Chet. "Tell us exactly what happened."

Chet related all he could remember.

"I didn't see the person well enough to identify him," he said ruefully. "But he sure fixed me up."

"You seem to be all right now," Joe remarked. "Maybe even a little fatter, as a matter of fact!"

"Say, I'm not so—" Chet began, patting his midriff. "Oh, I almost forgot!"

Grinning as he unbuttoned his jacket, Chet brought out a thick record book which had been hidden against his stomach.

"I was going through the papers," he explained. "I had just come across this book when I heard the noise, so I stuck it under my coat. Dilleau's name is in it," Chet added proudly.

"Great work!" Joe applauded, and Frank praised, "Chet, you're an ace!" He slapped his friend's shoulder.

"Some of the stuff about Dilleau was washed out by the fire-extinguisher liquid," Chet told them, "but part of it's left."

"Never mind, we'll take the records to our lab and try to restore them by special chemical treatment," Joe told him enthusiastically.

Overjoyed that something had been saved from the marauder who had rendered Chet unconscious, the Hardys took the charred book from the shed, locked it in the trunk of their car, and returned to the school. To their surprise, Mrs. Teevan was back and breakfast was ready. As they headed for the dining room, the boys met Greg Woodson, who wore an annoyed expression.

"That phone call requesting me to go back to college was a fake!" he informed them. "I'd sure like to know who sent me on that wild-goose chase."

"I wonder if Kurt might have done it to get you out of the way while he was having a lot of old records burned," Frank said, and told Greg about the "celebration."

"Well, he won't catch me off guard again," Greg said firmly. "I'm sticking right here!"

After breakfast, Frank told him that he and Joe planned to go home to work in their laboratory and try to restore and decipher the old data about Dilleau. Chet said he would leave too.

"I'll stay here and keep an eye on Kurt," Greg promised. "This time I won't leave!"

When the Hardys climbed into their car a little later, Frank could not get any response from the motor.

"The gas gauge!" he exclaimed, pointing to the *empty* reading. "But I filled the tank yesterday!"

"Somebody must have siphoned off the gasoline," Joe surmised. "Maybe we can borrow another car."

When they tried to start Greg's car they discovered that it, too, had no gas.

"Someone doesn't want us to leave here," Frank said grimly. "First they don't want us to stay, then they don't want us to go."

"Maybe the Yellow Feather found out we're going to try restoring the records about Harris Dilleau," Joe suggested.

"Which makes it look as if he might be the Yellow Feather," Joe conjectured.

"All the more reason for us getting home to our lab as fast as possible," Frank said. "But the question is, how?"

Joe grinned, then mentioned Chet's new contraption. It was better than walking! Taking the records from the car trunk, they went to find Chet. Fortunately, he had not left.

Chet wagged his head in pleased consent when they asked him for a ride. "So you had to fall back on my propeller sled, eh?" he said with an uproarious laugh. But upon learning that the boys' car and Greg's had been drained of fuel, he sobered. "That mysterious guy won't leave us alone a minute."

The three boys hurried to the river where Chet's invention was lashed to the school dock. Frank and Joe began to slip the lines that held it secure, and Chet spun the flywheel.

BOOM!

The concussion of the explosion that followed nearly knocked all three of them over. As they regained their balance, Frank asked, "What happened?"

Still a little groggy, Chet started to examine his motorized sled.

"The muffler," he said in a sorrowful voice, "has been blown to bits."

Parts of the cylindrical noise absorber were scattered over a wide area of ice.

"Someone put an explosive mixture in it," Chet groaned. "Benny Tass, I'll bet."

Chet wound the rope around the flywheel again and tugged. To his amazement, the motor caught hold and burst into a throaty roar.

"We may be driven deaf, but I'll get you fellows to Bayport," he yelled against the din as the three climbed aboard.

Once they picked up speed, the noise seemed to lessen. Since the motor was behind them, part of the racket was carried away to the rear.

"I'd sure like to know who wrecked my muffler," Chet grumbled. "Maybe it wasn't Benny after all. Kurt's mad enough at all of us to have done it."

As Joe remarked that he doubted that the headmaster would stoop to anything so childish, Frank's thoughts about the man were concentrating along other lines. Finally he said:

"You know, Skinny Mason once told us that Kurt was an expert on spring propulsion. I'd forgotten all about it until now. I wonder if that dart which knocked you out, Chet—"

"You mean he has invented some kind of noiseless pistol to fire darts?" Chet exploded.

"Exactly. And a large one that sent those harpoons out on the bay. That would account for the funny *twang* we heard."

The others gasped.

"I'm glad the regular cook came back," Chet said, turning a little pale. "No more meals for me at

Woodson Academy. And you fellows had better stay away from there too."

"Thanks for the advice," Joe said. "You know we won't take it."

"Well, advice doesn't cost anything," Chet remarked. "But I'd hate to spend any money on trying to keep you Hardys from sticking to a mystery until it's solved."

Since the Morton farm was nearer than the brothers' home, Chet planned to go there, then drive Frank and Joe to their house in his father's car. But the idea of a minute's stop was sidetracked when two pretty girls opened the door for them.

"It's about time," Callie and Iola chorused in mock severity. "We've been trying to find you all over town!"

"What's doing?" Joe grinned at Iola.

"Have you forgotten that tonight's the big sleigh ride?" she demanded.

Frank's jaw fell. "We were so tied up with this Yellow Feather mystery we never gave it a thought," he said apologetically to Callie.

"Well, we have it all arranged," she said. "Old Mr. Kemper is going to take us in his big sleigh." And then the girls told of the plans they had made.

"If we're going on a sleigh ride"—Frank finally broke up the banter—"you and I had better get home and do some work, Joe."

The Hardys departed, with Chet driving them in the Morton car.

At their home Frank and Joe were greeted in the hall by a peppery voice:

"Well, it's a pity you're never around when you're wanted!"

"Hello, Aunt Gertrude." Joe laughed. "Maybe we ought to have cards printed—*At Home Tuesdays!*"

"It would be a fine idea," his aunt snapped. "Then your visitors would know when to find you."

"Visitors? Did we have a visitor?" Frank asked seriously.

"Yes, indeed, but he couldn't wait. I gave him what he had come for. He said to tell you that Benny Tass had called!"

CHAPTER XIX

The Wild Chase

"BENNY TASS!" Joe exclaimed. "What did he want?"

"Oh, it had nothing to do with you boys," Aunt Gertrude told them. "He just asked for you first, that's all. He hasn't been gone long."

"But what was he after?" Frank persisted.

Before answering, Miss Hardy took a moment to chide him for his impatience, then at last went into details.

"Benny simply wanted the Woodson Academy annual for the year in which your father was graduated. He explained to me—very nicely, I might add —that there was no copy of that year's book at school."

"But what was his reason?" Joe asked.

"The boy explained that he was writing a story for the school's monthly bulletin about famous old Woodson athletes. Your father was one of the best that ever played in sports there, so naturally some facts about him should be included."

"You gave him the book?" Frank asked.

"Why, certainly! Would you want your father's name omitted from a story like that?"

Frank had to agree on that point but added, "I'm not sure Benny gave you the real reason why he wanted to get his hands on Dad's yearbook."

Aunt Gertrude bristled. "You mean he wasn't telling the truth? There was another reason?"

The boys told her of their search to make the strange cutout sheets fit over various book pages to reveal an important message.

"Kurt probably sent Benny here on the errand," Frank said. "We don't trust those two. Kurt may have found out that the message is in Dad's yearbook!"

"Then I'm going to march right out to Woodson Academy and get it back," Aunt Gertrude declared, and started for the hall closet to get her coat and hat.

The boys looked at each other and Joe winked. "It's a long, cold walk out there," he teased.

"Don't be impudent," his aunt said. "I'll take your father's car."

"We'll save you the trouble," Frank offered, going up to his aunt and giving her a hug. "And we won't tell Dad you gave away that book with all his pictures in it."

"Oh, you boys!" Miss Hardy exclaimed, trying to appear stern, but her affection for them got the better of her and she kissed them both. "Now get going," she said, "and bring that yearbook back before your father comes home! Benny was driving. Maybe you can catch him."

As the brothers ran toward the garage for Mr. Hardy's car, Joe said, "Now I'm sure it was Benny who drained the gas out of our car. He didn't want us to get here before he did!"

"Right."

The side door to the garage was ajar. Frank dashed through it, while Joe rolled up the big front doors.

"Phew! Smell that gasoline!" Frank called, then suddenly realized what the heavy odor meant. "Joe, the gas in this tank has been siphoned off, too!"

Both boys stood dismayed for a couple of seconds, fearful that more than this might have been done to the car. There was only one thing to do—roll it outside and examine the motor.

Quickly they pushed the sedan to the driveway. Frank unfastened the hood and looked inside, while Joe peered underneath and also inspected the trunk compartment.

"Looks okay," Joe reported.

"Same here," Frank said. "There's an emergency can of gas in the garage. Enough to get us started."

Joe raced inside for it and quickly emptied the contents into the tank. There was only one quart!

"It'll be enough to get us to a gas station, at least," he assured Frank. "The only trouble is we're losing

precious time. We'll never be able to catch Benny
—not the way he drives."

"We're going to try," Frank replied grimly as he
jumped into the driver's seat.

A few seconds later the motor purred to life and
the boys started off. They paused at a gas station
long enough to half fill the tank, then they were
off. Frank drove as fast as he dared on the snow-
packed roads.

"Say, I just realized," Joe suddenly spoke up,
"that in all the times we've driven this trip we've
never taken the short cut to the Academy."

"Where is it?"

"About a mile farther up this road you cut over
the lane on old Mr. Apperson's farm. It's a rough
road, but I think it's a lot shorter than this route."

"It's worth trying," Frank decided, and when the
intersection was reached, he turned off the main
highway and sent the car bouncing over the rutted
lane.

"Whoof!" Frank gasped as they jounced along.
"You weren't kidding about its being r-r-rough!
Just hope we don't break a spring!"

To their dismay the road did not improve as they
continued down its straight but bumpy length.

"Hey! Look out!" Joe cried.

The car hit an exceptionally bad rut and veered
crazily to one side. Frank spun the wheel helplessly
as the sedan went into a full skid. There was another

bad bump, then a jarring impact as the car shuddered to a halt in a ditch at the side of the road.

"Whew!" Joe said.

The boys sat still a few seconds to recover, then got out. After taking note of the car's position they concluded that it would be impossible to push it back on the road.

"I'll get the shovel and sand out of the rear compartment," Joe offered.

Mr. Hardy always carried this emergency equipment for winter driving, and his foresight proved to be a godsend. With Joe throwing sand over the slippery surface, Frank was able to drive the car back onto the road. This time he managed to stay in the hump-backed lane, and before long cut back onto the main highway.

"We did gain time, at that!" Frank exclaimed, looking at his watch. "Maybe we can catch up to Benny after all." He urged the car faster along the road to Woodson.

Five minutes later Joe cried excitedly, "There's a car up ahead! It might be Benny's!"

Foot by foot, they gained on the other vehicle. Obviously its driver did not realize that he was being chased, or he might have put on more speed.

"It's Tass, all right!" Joe said gleefully, as they neared the car ahead.

"I'm going to force him to the side and make him stop," Frank said.

He pulled up in back of Benny and then swung

alongside him. When the bully saw the Hardys, he made a desperate effort to get away, giving his motor full power. But the acceleration was fatal on the snowy road, and as his wheels spun madly Frank edged in front of him, forcing the youth to stop.

"What's the big idea?" Benny yelled angrily as the brothers hopped out and strode over to him.

"You have Dad's yearbook," Joe answered. "We want it back."

"Your aunt lent it to me," Benny snapped. "Isn't that good enough for you?"

"No, it's not," Frank said coldly. "Hand it over, Benny—right now."

"Wait a second, will you?" The bully dropped his blustering tone a little. "We just want to get some material out of it, that's all."

"Who's 'we'?" Frank inquired. "You and who else?"

"Why, Kurt. He's going to read it," Benny faltered.

"Nothing doing," Joe insisted. "Give it to me, Benny."

For a moment the bully fumed, his face red with anger. Then, apparently, he decided there was nothing he could do with the odds so decidedly against him but return the borrowed annual.

"Okay, if that's the way you feel about it," he said in a surly tone.

With that he picked up the book from the seat and started to hand it over. But as Joe reached through the window to take it, Benny's other hand flashed to the dashboard. In one movement he yanked out the ash tray full of cigarette refuse and emptied it into Joe's face! With a yelp of pain the boy fell back, trying to wipe the ashes from his eyes.

Benny, with a clashing of gears, gunned his motor.

"Oh, no, you don't!" Frank cried and dived through the window to take control.

One twist of the steering wheel and the car was off the road and on the soft shoulder in deep snow. Then Frank snapped off the ignition.

"Listen, you wise guy—" Benny stormed as he pushed open the door. "I've taken about enough of your meddling. You're going to get it now!"

He drove a vicious right to Frank's jaw, but the boy dodged and the blow whistled through the air! He stepped inside a wild swing from Benny's left so that it carried harmlessly over his shoulder.

Then Frank staggered his adversary with a smashing right jab to the solar plexus. As Benny doubled over, Frank caught him with a well-timed left hook to the chin! Dazed, the bully fell to the snow.

"Attaboy, Frank!" Joe cried as he took in the short-lived battle through blinking, watering eyes. "That's the way to handle a sneak!"

"Now get the book, Joe," Frank said as he stood over the beaten Benny.

Tass said nothing, holding his jaw in disgust as he watched Joe retrieve the yearbook. Then, using some of their sand, the Hardys put Benny's car back on the road. He still glowered at them as they drove off.

Eager to get started on the processing of the burnt record books, Frank and Joe returned home, ate a quick lunch, and then hurried into the workshop over the garage. After several hours the boys had failed to find a chemical combination which would restore the writing on the charred, damp pages. Disappointed, they were roused from their work by laughter below the laboratory window. Then heavy footsteps sounded on the stairs.

"Come on. Open up!" someone shouted.

"It's Chet! We forgot all about the sleigh ride," Joe groaned as he looked around at their half-completed work. "It must be six o'clock."

He opened the lab door and faced Chet and Callie.

"I don't know whether we can go after all," Frank began, stepping to the door. He looked apologetically at the girl. "We hate to pass up all this fun, but you see, this is really business—"

"Frank Hardy"—Callie shook her finger in mock anger—"this is one time when pleasure comes before business. You have a date!"

Frank winked at his brother. "What say, Joe— think we can give up our sleuthing for a few hours?" he asked with a chuckle.

"Let's go!" Joe grinned. "This problem will still be here for us tomorrow!"

In a few minutes the boys had cleaned up the lab and put on their lumberjackets and boots. Then, with Chet and Callie, they hurried out to the waiting sleigh. Climbing aboard, the Hardys were greeted heartily by Iola and half a dozen other friends who made up the party.

With all the happy group snuggled in the deep straw, old Mr. Kemper flicked the reins and the two horses broke into a trot. Smoothly the sleigh glided along and for half an hour the crisp night air echoed with the laughter and joking of the young people.

Just then Frank and Joe noticed that Mr. Kemper was heading the sleigh toward the Woodson Academy land.

"Say," Joe whispered excitedly to his brother, "we're not far away from the school shack. Wonder if there's any activity there tonight?"

"You mean—by the Yellow Feather?"

"Sure. I know! We could take a swing over that way and investigate," Joe suggested eagerly.

Before Frank could reply, Callie broke in.

"What *is* this about investigating yellow feathers?" she demanded.

"It's *the* Yellow Feather," Joe said. "It's somebody we'd like to catch—and he might be right around here, too."

"Want to help us?" Frank asked.

"No, thank you," Callie retorted. "Sounds too scary to me."

By this time everyone in the party was listening to the conversation with avid interest.

Biff Hooper spoke up. "I like to see the Hardy detective team at work on a case."

Frank and Joe needed little urging to oblige and soon were directing Mr. Kemper along the road that led to the stone cabin.

"Of course we might not find anything at all," Frank murmured to Joe as they neared the place.

For answer, Joe gripped his brother's arm and pointed as the hut came into view.

"Frank! There's a light inside. Someone *is* there!"

CHAPTER XX

A Frightened Bully

"WE'D BETTER stop here," Frank called to Mr. Kemper. "I don't want to get so close to the cabin that we'll be heard."

When the driver had reined in, Frank vaulted out of the sleigh, landing noiselessly in the deep snow.

"Joe! Chet! We'd better go the remainder of the way on foot," he whispered. "The rest of you stay here, and please be as quiet as possible."

"Do be careful!" Callie cautioned the boys.

"It's so spooky!" Iola shuddered.

Thrilled to see the Hardys in action, their friends promised to remain quiet. They sat in the sleigh and watched in the moonlight as the brothers and Chet moved off among the trees in the direction of the light from the cabin windows.

Soundlessly the trio crept up to the building. Flattening themselves against the stonework just below one of the windows, they listened. Two people were evidently arguing.

Henry Kurt and Benny Tass!

"Why did you let them get the book away from you?" Kurt was raging.

Benny's answer was not audible to those outside.

"Speak up!" Kurt stormed, his voice rising even higher. "What's the matter with you?"

"My jaw aches!" Tass complained. "It hurts to talk."

Frank glanced at Joe and Chet and grinned. He was just in time to catch Chet opening his mouth for the beginning of a loud horselaugh. Quickly he clapped his hand over his friend's face and muffled the guffaw.

"*S-sh*—don't give us away!" he warned.

Inside, Kurt was talking again. "Listen here," he ordered. "You go back and get that book or there'll be trouble. And this time no excuses!"

"But how am I going to get it?" Benny whined. "The Hardy boys have probably warned their family not to give it to me and they're certainly not going to hand it over."

Kurt sneered. "I thought you wanted to help me in return for some—er—favors I've done for you."

"Yes, I know," Benny quavered. "But you'd better do this job yourself."

"How dumb can you be?" Kurt snorted in disgust. "I said, get that yearbook!"

"You mean you want me to break into the Hardy

house?" Benny asked in disbelief. "And steal the yearbook?'"

"All I'm telling you," Kurt said in a chilling tone, "is to get that book back before the Yellow Feather catches up with you!"

"Yes, sir, yes, sir." The rest of Benny's reply was such an indistinct mumble that the listeners outside could not make it out.

There were footsteps across the floor and the squeaking of a door.

"Get back!" Frank warned Joe and Chet just in time.

The door opened and a stream of yellow light fell across the snow. In its path the three boys saw Benny Tass appear, his head hanging, his shoulders slumped. Behind him, in the doorway, stood Kurt, an arrogant, dominant figure.

"Remember what I told you," he bit off in a cold, impersonal voice. "It'll make a difference in your school marks and—er—your scholarship!"

Then the door slammed, and Benny was left alone. For a moment he stood in the shadow of the shack, evidently undecided what to do. Finally he dragged himself off.

"Go after him!" Frank whispered to Joe and Chet. "I'll check on Kurt."

Stealthily the two boys followed the bully into the woods. He was plodding along, kicking at the snow and muttering to himself. When Joe and Chet were out of earshot of the cabin, Joe called out:

"Benny! Wait for us!"

With a start, Tass whirled around. It was evident the last persons he expected to see in the woods at this moment were Joe Hardy and Chet Morton.

"Wh-what are you guys doing here?" he gasped.

"We happened to be going by with some friends," Joe told him. "When we saw a light in the cabin, we thought we'd do a little investigating."

"You've been spying!"

"Detective work includes that," Joe said frigidly. "After all, we're supposed to be tracking down the Yellow Feather. It was Kurt's guess that he hangs around the cabin, so you can't blame us for looking here."

Benny seemed frightened, not so much by Joe's presence as by the mention of the Yellow Feather.

"Did you hear what Kurt said in there?" he asked.

"Part of it."

"The part about the Yellow Feather—and getting the yearbook back?"

The boys nodded, and Joe asked, "When are you going to get smart, Benny?"

"What do you mean?"

"I mean when are you going to stop playing stooge for Kurt? Can't you see he's just using you to do his dirty work? All you get out of it are good marks and some sports medals. And you're taking a chance on going to jail!"

"Oh, no, not that!" Benny cried in alarm.

"Sure," Chet followed up the warning. "Kurt's

going to pin all the blame on you when the time comes."

Tass stood sullenly tracing patterns in the snow with one foot and seemed to be considering the advice.

"How'd you get mixed up with Kurt?" Joe asked him.

"I wanted to solve the mystery," came the startling answer. "I thought I could beat you fellows to it."

Then the whole story came out, the words tumbling over themselves in Benny's eagerness to confide in someone.

"Kurt told me about the mystery before you guys ever showed up. He said that I could help in return for the scholarship. I thought I was going to catch the Yellow Feather myself, until you Hardys came along. When I heard that Greg Woodson asked you up to his room, I fixed that wire in the hallway so I could listen without being caught."

Joe clenched his fists and flushed with anger, but realized he must remain calm to get more information out of Benny.

"Were you the one who started to climb the ladder into our room?"

"Yes. I planned to play a gag on you that would scare you off the case," Benny admitted sheepishly. "But something happened to the ladder, and I took a mean flop. I got in your room later, but because I was seen by one of the fellows I couldn't do what I planned. So I just took your brother's pants and threw them on the tower."

"Someone pulled the ladder away," Joe said. "You don't know who it was?"

"No."

Chet looked at him severely.

"Did you have anything to do with knocking me out in the tool house and painting a yellow feather on the side of it?"

Benny looked frightened. "No. Honestly I didn't have a thing to do with that. Outside of what I've told you, the only thing I did was try to shove you off the road one night. Kurt was with me and suggested it."

Joe looked straight at Benny. "Are you going to wake up now and quit playing on Kurt's side? Or will you carry out his orders and try to steal the yearbook from our house?"

Benny's jaw dropped at this disclosure. Joe knew that he had scored a strong point in his argument.

"I know a cop," Chet added, "who will keep a close watch on your house, Joe."

Benny scuffed the snow even harder.

"Cut it out, Morton. You're not scaring me. I'm not afraid of cops. About Kurt, though, I don't know. I'm getting sick and tired of having him push me around."

"How would you like to help us instead of him?" Joe suggested with a grin. "First of all, have you any idea who the Yellow Feather is?"

"Yes, I do," Benny answered and enjoyed the others' expressions of complete astonishment. "And if you hadn't come here and messed things up, I'd have caught him myself, too."

"Who is he?" Joe demanded.

Benny began to hedge. "I don't know exactly, but he's somebody under twenty-one years of age, I guess, from what Kurt said about him. At least, Kurt once made a crack about the Yellow Feather being a minor."

"So Kurt has been holding out on some information from Mr. Hardy?" Chet remarked in disgust.

"I don't believe the Yellow Feather's a person under twenty-one," Joe commented. "Why would anyone so young want to inherit a school which is practically running in the red?"

"Anyway," Benny went on, "the Yellow Feather's someone who has it in for the Woodson family."

"Go ahead," Joe prodded. "What else do you know, Benny?"

But that, the youth declared, was all he could tell about the mysterious enemy, and no amount of interrogation could draw more information from him. Finally, at the urging of Joe and Chet, Benny agreed to work with them, and if Kurt became too tough on him, to come to them for assistance. He promised to go back to the Academy at once and retire for the night. After he was out of sight, Chet remarked:

"I really think Benny will be all right from now on, Joe."

"If so, it'll be a relief," Joe answered. "There'll be one less obstacle to overcome."

"Say," said Chet, "what did you think about his ideas on the Yellow Feather? Could this mystery man be a former student at the Academy? A crank who's been holding onto a grudge that he'd built up here?"

"Could be," Joe agreed, as both boys cautiously headed for the cabin.

Frank, meanwhile, had been spying at the cabin. When Kurt had gone back inside, the young detective had crawled to a position under one of the windows. Now his eyes were on a level with the sill.

Kurt stood at the table in the center of the room, his back to the boy. He seemed to be studying some papers, moving them here and there about the table. Were they schoolwork, Frank wondered, or were they plans for a new invention that the headmaster was working on? Suddenly Kurt turned partly around, holding one paper up as if for better illumination.

It was a sheet of white letter paper with rectangular cutouts!

As Frank watched, his heart pounding, Kurt replaced the perforated sheet on the table. Then, with a sweep of his hands, he collected all of the other papers into one batch and dropped them into the fireplace. A flick of a match, and they were ablaze.

"What is he up to?" Frank asked himself as Kurt again picked up the cutout paper and approached the fireplace. Surely he was not going to burn it! If he threw it into the fireplace, Frank was determined to rescue the paper!

But this was not Kurt's intention. With one hand he raised the top of the mantelpiece. With the other he carefully tucked the paper beneath the lid and closed it. Then he turned out the kerosene lantern which was the room's only light.

Backing away from the window, Frank nearly ran into Joe and Chet as they came up behind him. With a motion of his hand, he stilled the questions on their lips. A second later Henry Kurt emerged from the cabin and stalked off into the darkness.

"Stand guard, will you?" Frank hissed to the others as he moved forward. "I'm going in!"

CHAPTER XXI

An Unexpected Twist

INSIDE the camp cabin, Frank raced across the room to the fireplace. Stomping with his heavy snow boots on what remained of the flames, he snuffed them out, then recovered what he could of the papers. Relighting the lantern, he studied the scraps.

"Book pages," Frank reflected.

Apparently they had been torn from many kinds of large-page books, covering a variety of subject matter with no significant relationship among the subjects. There was only one similarity in the sheets —they were all exactly the same size.

"Kurt was probably trying to fit that cutout page over them," the young sleuth deduced. "And since he tossed them all into the fire, none of them could have been the one he was looking for."

Nevertheless, Frank spread the salvaged papers on the cabin table. Then he reached into the space under the movable mantel and lifted out the perforated sheet.

Was this the original letter from old Elias Woodson to Greg? There was no telling. Greg himself would have to answer that.

But as Frank studied it, he noted definitely that the size of the rectangular cutouts and the spacing between them were completely different from those on the other two sheets he had seen.

"All our work in the Academy library for nothing," the boy thought ruefully.

At this moment Joe burst impatiently through the cabin doorway. "What's going on?" he cried.

Learning that Chet was still on guard, Frank quickly explained all that he had seen through the window and what he had just found. Joe carefully examined the cutout paper. Then he held it up to the light.

"It looks older than the copy Kurt gave Dad," Joe remarked. "And say, here's a mark that wasn't on the other."

Scratched on the paper, evidently with a fingernail, and visible only when looked at against the light were two letters: EW.

Elias Woodson!

"This paper is the real thing!" Frank exclaimed excitedly. "Kurt must have found it on the river after Greg dropped it."

"He has done us a great favor without meaning to," Joe said with a grin. "We'll take this along."

"And leave a fake copy here," said Frank, "so when Kurt comes back for the paper, he won't be disappointed—or suspicious."

"Good idea!" Joe agreed. "And we'll put the cut-outs just enough out of line so it won't do him any good."

Suddenly Frank's exuberance changed to a note of seriousness. "Just where are we going to find the paper to use for the substitute?" he asked.

The brothers searched the cabin for a similar sheet without success. Next, Frank examined the papers he had rescued from the fire. Finally he held up an undamaged blank page. Though slightly smaller and heavier, it was not so unlike the genuine one that Kurt would immediately notice the change.

"By the time Kurt discovers the switch, it won't matter, anyhow," said Frank.

Joe took out his pocketknife, and with its small blade carefully marked small rectangles on the sheet and then gently punched them out. In a few minutes the job was done. He rubbed his hands back and forth over it several times to give the paper a slightly mussed-up appearance, then handed it to Frank.

"Perfect!" his brother said.

He folded the sheet in exactly the same way that the original had been creased. Lifting the top of the mantelshelf, he inserted the fake document in the secret hiding place.

"Now we'll finish the burning job that Kurt started," Frank said as he threw the rest of the odd papers into the fireplace and set fire to them. "Kurt will never know anyone was here."

"Unless Benny Tass tells him!" Joe remarked. He reported the talk that he and Chet had had with the bully.

"Maybe Benny will reform," Frank said hopefully. "Well, we'll soon know. But in any case, we have the lost paper."

After putting the precious sheet into an inside pocket of his jacket, Frank led the way outside.

When Chet had been brought up to date on the news he whistled gleefully.

"Looks like things are closing in on our friend Kurt," he chortled.

The three boys trudged through the snow to where their friends still waited in Mr. Kemper's sleigh.

"Where are all the bad men?" Iola teased the returning sleuths. "Why, we expected to see you leading a chain gang of handcuffed prisoners that you'd captured barehanded!"

"My gloves got in the way," Joe replied, grinning.

"You didn't bring even one little crook?" Callie pretended to be amazed.

"Only this hefty guard," Frank answered, boosting Chet into the sleigh. "He's carrying all the hidden gold on him and will pay for everyone's supper."

"Hurrah!" all of them except Chet shouted.

That youth cried, "Hey, wait a minute! I—" But no one paid any attention to him.

Mr. Kemper, as previously arranged, drove his passengers to an old inn owned by relatives of one of the girls. The young people spent a hilarious evening, relishing the fine food for which the place was famous and singing and dancing to the latest hit-tune records.

The singing continued on the trip home, the sweet harmonies filling the crisp night air as the sleigh jingled along the country roads. The Hardys thoroughly enjoyed every minute of it, but as soon as they returned to Bayport as they had planned, and the quiet of their room at home, the boys again discussed the subject foremost in their minds.

"I meant to tell you," Joe reported, "what Benny said about the Yellow Feather. Kurt knows who he is."

"What!"

Joe repeated Tass's theory that the Yellow Feather must be under twenty-one years of age, because Kurt had once spoken of him as being a minor.

"A minor?" Frank puzzled. "Well, he certainly pulled some acts of advanced crime for a young man —knocking you cold and leaving you in that boathouse, shooting at us with a harpoon gun, and conking Chet with that dart."

"Wait a minute!" Joe cried. "I wonder if Benny misunderstood Kurt? Did he mean *miner* instead of minor—is there a mine mixed up in this case?"

That was a new angle, and the boys discussed it excitedly.

"Greg hasn't mentioned anything about a mine," Frank mused. "On the other hand, maybe he doesn't know about it. Elias Woodson may have owned some stock in one."

"If the stock has any value, it could be the real reason why the Yellow Feather—and Kurt—are making such a big thing out of the inheritance," Joe offered.

"What kind of mine could it be?" Frank reflected, "and where is it?"

"I think those cutouts might give us the answer," Joe replied. "I'd like to get to work on it now, but I suppose we should get some sleep."

Flipping the light switch, he moved to the window to open it for the night. As he did, a vague, almost indiscernible shifting of shadows below caught his attention.

Frozen in his tracks, Joe stared hard at the moonlit scene outside. Not one, but two figures were moving in the dark protection of the trees and hedges.

Joe called to Frank, who was out of bed and at his side in an instant. One figure was close to the house now, almost under their window. The other seemed to be following him.

"Out the back door!" Frank suggested.

In a flash, the brothers were rushing barefoot down the back stairs. Just before opening the door, they looked out a window. The moon had gone under a cloud. The two figures had halted and the one nearer the house seemed to be trying to make up his mind what to do.

"Joe, I'll sneak out and tackle the second figure," Frank offered. "When you see me tackle him, snap on the porch light and nab the first fellow!"

"Okay."

They opened the door silently and Frank padded softly along the edge of the back porch in the shadows, while Joe stood poised with his hand on the light switch.

A moment later Frank made a headlong tackle for his man. Joe snapped on the light and went after the other!

CHAPTER XXII

A Startling Story

FRANK's slashing tackle crashed the silent figure to the ground. The man rolled with the force of the boy's dive, then bounced to his feet.

"Dad!" Frank cried as he recognized his intended captive in the light from the porch. "I'm sorry. I—"

At this outburst Joe, stunned, stopped his chase of the other man momentarily. He might be a friend of his father's coming to spend the night. But this idea was instantly dispelled when the man made a beeline for the street.

"Joe, go after that snooper!" Mr. Hardy yelled.

Joe dashed toward the front of the house where the intruder had fled. His father and Frank followed. But the stranger had vanished.

"You fellows get back into the house," Mr. Hardy ordered as he noted that they were shivering. "I'll scout around the neighborhood and see if I can find any trace of that prowler."

As Frank and Joe ran inside they were met by

Mrs. Hardy and Aunt Gertrude. Both women wanted to know what had happened. Upon learning that the prowler had not entered the house, the boys' mother sighed in relief and said she would fix hot cocoa for them and Mr. Hardy.

Aunt Gertrude, however, burst into a tirade. "Burglar or no burglar," she said sternly to her nephews. "The idea of your running out in pajamas in the middle of the night! And in bare feet! You'll probably have chilblains. Go right up and get under a hot shower. No, don't do that. You put snow on frozen feet."

"You mean you want us to go out again?" Joe grinned, but as his aunt withered him with a look, he added, "Don't worry. We weren't out long enough to join the Polar Club."

By the time the steaming cocoa was ready, Mr. Hardy was back. He reported that the intruder had made a clean getaway. Then he looked at Frank.

"That was a great tackle you made, son." He laughed. "I see why Bayport High racked up a score of victories in the past three years."

"How did you happen to be trailing that man?" Frank asked him.

"I was taking a short cut home," Mr. Hardy answered, "when I saw somebody slip across the hedge at the rear and head for the house. Naturally I followed, and was just about ready to challenge him when Frank hit me at the five-yard line and threw me for a loss."

"It's too bad I picked on the wrong team," Frank said ruefully.

Mrs. Hardy served cocoa and cookies to the entire family. As they ate, Frank and Joe reviewed for the others the latest developments in the case—the chase after Benny and the yearbook, the clue of the miner, and the recovery of what seemed to be the original cutout sheet.

"Tomorrow we'll go back to the Woodson library with the sheet and start looking again for a clue," Joe told them.

"And in Dad's yearbook, too," Frank added.

Suddenly the older detective's eyes lighted up. "Boys," he said, "I believe you've solved this mystery!"

Frank and Joe stared at him for a moment in astonishment. "How?" they asked together.

"Let me see that sheet," Mr. Hardy requested. "And bring that yearbook down with you too."

"Sure thing," Frank dashed from the kitchen and ran upstairs for the two articles. In a moment the detective was flipping through the yearbook's pages, with his sons looking over his shoulders. As he paused to gaze at a certain page, the boys saw a picture of Mr. Hardy in a Woodson basketball uniform. The yearbook also carried a short account of his prowess on the court.

"Here it is!" their father exclaimed. He directed his fingers to two words in the third and fourth lines. "I just remembered this!"

"Yellow Feather!" the boys cried unbelievingly. "You—you—"

"No, I'm not the Yellow Feather," Mr. Hardy hastened to say.

"Well, I should hope not!" Aunt Gertrude bristled. "The idea!"

"I believe," Mr. Hardy went on, "that Elias Woodson's message to Greg is in this article. That's why he printed the word Hardy on the corner of the perforated sheet."

Deftly the detective placed the sheet of paper with the cutouts over the page. With a pencil he drew sharp black lines around the words and parts of words that were showing. Everyone waited breathlessly to see what the message would be. When Mr. Hardy removed the sheet, the page looked as follows:

FENTON HARDY

Woodson's high-scoring forward set the pace with 26 points to help the /Yellow/ and Black beat Craigly. Another /feather/ in Hardy's cap was the /gold/en opportunity he seized to sink the winning basket that deter/mine/d the state championship one week later. /Man/ of the year /i/n athletics. /To/ the /Ba/yport ace and our winning team, congratulations!

Quickly Frank read aloud the special message of the ringed words:

"*Yellow Feather Gold Mine Manitoba.*"

"Then there is a mine—a gold mine in Canada!" Joe cried. "Wait until Greg hears this!"

"Yes, but we must be careful about telling him," Mr. Hardy cautioned both his sons. "One thing I'm sure of. Even if Kurt knows there's a mine, he doesn't know where it is and we don't want him to get any inkling of the location."

"After that prowler's visit—and I believe it might have been Kurt—we'd better lock both the paper and the book in your safe, Dad," Frank advised.

"We'll do it at once," said Mr. Hardy, rising from the kitchen chair. After thanking Mrs. Hardy for the midnight snack, he and the boys went upstairs. "When you tell Greg about the mine," the detective warned them, "be sure there are no eavesdroppers around."

Joe remarked that the easiest way out would be to have Kurt arrested. Surely it was plain he was trying to steal the Woodson estate.

"We don't have enough on him yet," Mr. Hardy reminded his son. "I'm just as sure as you are that he's mixed up in the case for selfish reasons, but we must let him tip his own hand."

"How?"

"Well, I'd guess Kurt is delaying a final move for two reasons. First, he knows about the mine—probably got that much out of Elias Woodson—but as I said, he doesn't know where it is. And secondly," the investigator pointed out, "he must find the old man's will and destroy it. Then, when there's no longer any danger that someone else will inherit the property, Kurt will produce a forged will, leaving everything to him, and pretend it has just been found."

"Pretty slick," Joe commented. "I can't wait to trip him up."

The three discussed means of halting Kurt's evil scheme. Mr. Hardy decided the best thing for him to do was fly to Manitoba and obtain firsthand information of the mine. He might even find that a lawyer in the province had a copy of the will.

"At least there must be some record of ownership out there which could be produced in court," the detective said. "In the meantime, you boys try to get some more information on Kurt's relationship with this fellow Dilleau," he suggested as the discussion broke up for the night.

By the time the boys arose the next morning, Mr. Hardy had already left for Manitoba on an early plane.

"We'd better get back to work on restoring that article about Dilleau," Frank decided, and as soon as breakfast was over, he and Joe headed for their laboratory in the garage loft.

Picking up the experiments that had been interrupted the night before, the boys again subjected the charred remains of the papers to various tests.

Finally, they found the right combination of chemicals.

"Look—some of the printing is reappearing!" Joe exulted as words and phrases began to show again on the scorched pages.

Bit by bit, the text filled in until most of the material on Harris Dilleau was again readable. The article had been published in one of the monthly school bulletins.

"So Dilleau was president of the school's Science Club," Frank remarked as he began to read. "Listen to this: 'An enthusiast who might some day blow up the world in his determination to perfect the secret formula he talks about.' "

"Nice guy to room with," Joe commented.

Frank went on reading. "Here it says Dilleau had a touch of genius. That's why he got such terrific grades in all the sciences."

As they finished reading they heard Aunt Gertrude's voice calling them to the telephone.

"I'll take it," Frank offered and hurried to the house. Returning a few minutes later, he said, "It was Chet."

"What did he want?"

"Asked us to help him put some kind of reverse gear on the engine of that propeller sled," Frank explained.

"What did Chet say when you told him that we couldn't help him?"

"He'll work on it by himself," Frank replied. "I

told him we were going back to the Academy and he offered to drive us out there in his jalopy."

"Swell, only I hope it gets us there."

Chet arrived fifteen minutes later to drive his friends to the campus. Squeezed in beside the stout youth, Frank and Joe clung to the sides and front of the topless car. Between the jouncing and the racket, conversation was impossible.

When they reached the Academy, the Hardys hopped out, thanked Chet, and hurried into the main building. First they checked on the whereabouts of the headmaster and learned from Mr. Teevan that Kurt had taken a party of younger boys some distance into the woods to build a snow fort. Benny Tass, too, was out of the building. The brothers mounted the stairs to see if Greg was in his room.

"We can talk to him without having Kurt or Benny spying on us," Joe remarked.

Fortunately, Greg was there. When informed of the discovery that the Yellow Feather was a gold mine and not a person, he gasped in amazement and wrung the brothers' hands in gratitude.

"If only it's a producing vein!" he cried, "I'll be able to use the money to put the school back on a paying basis. It would be a good idea to get the word around right away, so that people will know we're going to have a top-flight Academy again!"

It took a great deal of dissuading on the part of the Hardys to check Greg's enthusiasm, reminding him that his grandfather's will must be found in order to prove ownership and that Mr. Hardy had gone to Manitoba to learn what he could. At last Greg agreed that secrecy would be the wiser tactic for the time being.

"What's the first move for us?" he asked.

"I think we should get in touch with Skinny's uncle—the one who was in Dilleau's class here," Frank proposed. "He may know something about him. If we could find Harris Dilleau and why he wanted revenge—"

"And," Joe took over, "if Dilleau is a friend of Kurt's—"

Luckily, Skinny had not left yet to help with the snow fort. He telephoned his uncle John Mason and after a few words turned the instrument over to Frank.

"Yes, I've heard rumors about Dilleau," Mr. Mason replied to the boy's first question. "Last I knew about him, his name had been added to a list of criminals wanted in his home state."

"He escaped from prison?" Frank gasped.

"Yes. He was in for a long term as a swindler but through some clever invention that had to do with spring propulsion he managed to escape."

"How long ago was that?" Frank questioned, his excitement mounting.

"Oh, about three years," Skinny's uncle replied. "Since then there hasn't been a trace of him. It's thought he may have fled the country."

Thanking Mr. Mason for his assistance, Frank

hung up and stepped outside the booth. Smiling at Skinny, he said:

"Your uncle was a great help. I guess that's all we need now. Don't you want to go out and help with the snow fort?"

"Yes, I do," the lad replied. "So long, fellows. Be seeing you."

After Skinny had gone, Frank repeated the telephone conversation to Joe and Greg, and added tersely:

"I'm sure now that Harris Dilleau and Henry Kurt are the same person!"

CHAPTER XXIII

Cannon Balls of Ice

GREG's face registered severe shock. "You mean a
hunted criminal is running this school?" he cried in
dismay. "I can't believe it."

"There are several reasons that point to it," Frank
said. "First, we know about Kurt's flair for inventing
things. He has a scientific mind, one of the best, according to the people here in the Academy."

"And so did Dilleau," Joe burst out in support of
his brother's theory. "That yearbook mentioned that
he was head of the Science Club."

Greg still was unconvinced, although he could see
the logic behind this connection.

"But what about pictures of him around?" he
asked. "Even though he's older, it wouldn't be too
hard to identify him and no one ever has."

"Don't forget," Joe said, "that as soon as Kurt
found out we'd seen him looking at the desk with
Harris D on it he ordered all the old records
burned."

"That's right," Greg conceded. "But I still can't see why the police wouldn't have recognized him," Greg said. "Kurt comes and goes freely. He certainly makes no attempt to disguise himself."

Frank threw another bombshell into the conversation by saying he thought Greg was wrong on this point. "All Kurt needed to do in order to hide his identity was to have a plastic surgery job and grow that goatee," he pointed out.

Greg, now that the case against Kurt looked so strong, was determined to call in the police. But again the Hardys tried to talk him out of a rash move.

"We haven't enough evidence yet for the police," Frank cautioned him. "We need more proof."

"Besides," Joe added, "how about the reputation of the school. Every pupil in the place might leave if the authorities came charging in here and caused a lot of unfavorable publicity."

"When Dad gets back," Frank suggested, "he can arrange it so that the whole deal will be taken care of quietly."

Greg was convinced, but he said he thought a day-and-night watch should be put on the headmaster. Frank thought this unnecessary. With the will missing, the man would not be likely to leave Woodson.

"But we might go and see what he's doing now. He may be up to something more than directing the building of a snow fort."

"Right."

Greg put on his heavy boots and jacket, then the three hurried outside. As they rounded the corner of the administration building a husky figure approached them.

"Get your guard up," Joe advised with a whisper. "Here comes Benny."

But the bully seemed to be in unusually good spirits.

"Hi, you guys!" he called as he approached. "What angles are you working on today?"

Warily Frank glanced at Joe. Had this boy really turned over a new leaf and joined their side? Frank decided to be sure before revealing any theories they had.

"Nothing much so far," he replied in as friendly a voice as he could manage. "The Yellow Feather still seems to be at large, unless you've caught him."

"Not me!" Benny exclaimed, with an involuntary glance behind him. "I'm not too anxious to catch up with that crook."

"Where are you heading now?" Joe asked, just to make conversation.

"Oh, I thought I'd go for a hike," Benny answered. "They say that's quite an ice fort the kids are building out in the woods. I thought I might watch them for a while."

Frank, wanting to keep a wary eye on Benny, suggested that they all walk over to the site at once. Deep in the woods, they came upon the nearly finished fort. Set back against a knoll, and surrounded by high trees, it looked unassailable.

"Those walls must be three feet thick," Joe said in amazement as he studied the snow fort.

"It looks more like a giant igloo than the kind of open snow fort we used to build when we were kids," Frank remarked, his attention focused on the vaulted roof which covered the entire structure.

Under Kurt's direction students were busy carrying buckets back and forth to a nearby stream. Through a hole chopped in the ice, each boy lowered his pail, filled it, emptied the contents on the fort, and returned for more water.

"The water freezes almost immediately," Greg noted as they watched the process. "The fort must be as hard as granite."

"There's Skinny Mason," Joe said as their young friend's head poked through the tiny opening that served as a door. "He must be working on the inside."

The entrance to the interior was a narrow slit in one side.

"I don't like the idea of him going in there," Frank commented.

"You don't think it will collapse, do you?" Greg asked.

"No, not that. But the whole thing is on the grim side. It's not like a play fort and the boys don't seem to be having much fun."

"It does have a creepy atmosphere about it," Joe agreed.

"Hey! Look at Kurt!" Benny spoke up. "He's moving up some kind of cannon he's going to shoot off."

As the Hardys turned, they saw the headmaster swing a harpoon gun around on its tripod. The Hardys exchanged significant glances, but the students shrieked in delight.

For instead of harpoons, Kurt was loading it with giant icicles! He took dead aim at the side of the fort and fired. There was a twanging, a sound now familiar to the brothers. One more bit of evidence against Kurt!

The spearlike weapon rocketed toward the fort and landed on the roof. Frank and Joe held their breaths wondering if the force of the impact would cause a partial cave-in on the boys inside. But the icicle hardly made a dent in the solid exterior.

Again and again, Kurt sent his "ammunition" screaming and whistling toward the fort. The giant icicles exploded into tiny, gleaming fragments as they hit.

Although several students asked to shoot off the gun, Kurt would not permit this. Eventually picking it up, he handed the weapon to two of the boys and ordered the whole group back to the Academy.

"But we haven't had a snowball fight," Skinny objected. "You promised—"

"It's too late," the headmaster replied sternly.

"Your lunch will be ready. Hurry now, all of you!"

Disappointed, the students marched sullenly back to the school. Frank and Joe, together with Greg and Benny, went forward to inspect the fort at close range.

"This is a masterpiece of engineering," Greg remarked.

"Can you imagine being trapped in a thing like this?" Frank asked. "If that door were ever sealed up, anyone inside would be a goner!"

"Just like a tomb," Benny agreed in awe. "Ugh! Let's get away from here."

The others smiled, wondering if Benny were fearful that they might play a joke on him. They could not resist the temptation to tease him.

"How about playing a little game?" Joe suggested.

"What kind of game?" Benny asked suspiciously.

"You go inside the fort, while Frank and I—" Joe began slowly.

"Not on your life," the bully interrupted.

"Afraid?" Frank gibed.

Benny gave him a withering look. "Of course not. It's just that I—well, I'm kind of chilly. I think I'd better get back to the dorm."

"Okay," Joe shrugged.

The other boy looked relieved. After a complete inspection of the fort, the four boys headed back to the school. To their surprise, Benny continued to be pleasant. When they reached the main building, he said good-by cordially.

"Thanks for letting me go along," he said. "I'll be seeing you soon."

He went up the stairs to his room.

"Looks as if reform is really taking hold," Joe commented.

"Hope it lasts," Frank grunted.

After lunch, Greg and the Hardys held a powwow on their next move and decided on going directly to the school library since no one would be in it at that time of day.

"This time we *must* find a clue," Greg said. "I'm worried that Kurt will somehow get ahead of us."

"I agree," said Frank.

Halfway up the stairs, Frank and Joe were interrupted by a student calling from below.

"Hey! You Hardys! There's a telephone call for you—long-distance! Make it snappy!"

"Dad!" the brothers said in unison as they turned and ran down the steps.

Together they squeezed into the telephone booth. Frank picked up the receiver.

"Person-to-person from Mr. Fenton Hardy to Frank or Joe Hardy," came the singsong voice of the operator.

"We're here!"

"Go ahead, please."

A few seconds went by as various operators relayed the call, then Mr. Hardy's voice came over the wire clear and strong. After a quick exchange of greetings, he reported on the work he was doing in Winnipeg.

"I've been talking to authorities up here about the location of the Yellow Feather Mine," he said. "They tell me that there isn't any such operation listed in the province, and no one has ever heard of it."

The boys' hearts sank. They asked him if the mine angle was a dud.

"No, not at all," Mr. Hardy assured them. "I was lucky enough to run into an elderly hotel man up here named Davis. He knew Elias Woodson well. He often stayed at the hotel. Woodson was very fond of this province, it seems. Davis said the old gentleman once told him that he owned a producing gold mine."

"Did he say where it was?" Frank asked eagerly.

"Yes. Colorado."

"Swell!" Joe cried. "Things are finally beginning to look up!"

"I'm going to fly to Colorado," Mr. Hardy said, "and find out what I can."

"When, Dad?"

"I'll leave here in a couple of hours," his father replied. "By the way, I almost forgot to tell you another interesting bit of information Mr. Davis gave me. The tower has a secret—"

"What kind of secret?" Frank asked in amazement as his father's voice suddenly broke off.

CHAPTER XXIV

Victory Snatched Away

"HELLO! Hello!" Frank shouted into the mouth-piece. "I was cut off, operator!"

But though she tried, the operator could not restore Mr. Hardy's connection from Winnipeg.

"Sorry," she said, and Frank hung up.

"I wonder what Dad was going to tell us," Joe pondered.

"All I could get was that the bell tower has some kind of secret," Frank murmured in disappointment. "Perhaps a hidden room."

"If we investigate it, maybe we can find out," Joe said eagerly.

It was arranged that Greg would keep tabs on the headmaster during the search. Fortunately, Kurt had locked himself in his office and did not reappear for a long while.

In the meantime, the Hardys went to the catwalk of the tower and looked at the exterior of the structure thoughtfully. From his former trip to the belfry Joe knew there was no visible entrance.

But there might be a concealed one.

"Surely when the original stairway was removed," he said, "some means of entrance must have been substituted."

"There should be some kind of door," Frank decided. "But why should they want to conceal it? Suppose something went wrong with the bell. How would they fix it?"

Every inch of the belfry wall was tapped and Frank even stood on Joe's shoulders to investigate in order not to miss any possibility.

"No go," he said finally. "If there's an entrance, it's somewhere inside the building. Maybe in the attic where the bell tower joins the roof."

For the first time the boys realized that the architecture of the building was a bit odd. The belfry was located where one wing joined the main part of the building.

"I think," said Frank, "that once upon a time the tower extended up on the outside of the main building and the wing was constructed around it."

"Then there might be an entrance to the old shaft in the cellar," Joe speculated.

The boys hurried to the basement, where the foundation of the circular structure was plainly visible. Furthermore, the section where a door into it had once been present was solidly bricked in with a lighter shade of mortar.

"Stymied again!" Joe said, dropping onto a nearby box.

Frank sat down beside his brother and for a few minutes both were lost in thought. What had their father discovered which they could not find? It was maddening not to be able to figure out the secret.

"I suppose," said Joe, rising, "that the thing to do is examine the tower where it passes through each floor."

The boys climbed to the ground level and marveled at the clever way the architect had covered up any evidence of the former tower. A series of cabinets with shelves, now filled with school supplies, hid the old structure.

"No entrance here," Frank muttered and started for the stairway.

The room adjoining the old tower shaft on the second floor was a large study hall, now vacant. The room was pine-paneled, whereas the other rooms had plastered walls. Both boys speculated about this curious change in the architect's plans.

I'll bet there's a secret panel here," Frank said, his interest renewed. "Keep watch in the hall, will you Joe, while I do some tapping?"

Inch by inch, Frank used his knuckles and finger tips on the wood. There were hollow and solid sounds but nothing moved or even vibrated. But he was so sure that the answer to the secret was here that he tried pushing sideways against the trim that covered the seams between the pine boards.

Suddenly he was rewarded. A section of the wall began to move!

"Joe! *S-s-st!*"

His brother came on the run and had to stifle a shout of glee. Frank said he was going inside. In the event that he could not get out, Joe was to use the same combination to open the door when Frank tapped on the panel.

"Give me ten minutes," Frank suggested and closed himself in.

Joe ambled back to the hall. To his consternation, Greg and Kurt were coming up the nearest stairway together. Joe walked toward them, pretending to be on his way down.

With a bare nod, Kurt brushed past him. Then, stiffly saying "Good-by" to Greg, the headmaster turned into the study hall.

Joe was aghast. He must get Kurt out of there at once! Frank might tap on the panel at any moment! He motioned to Greg to wait.

"Oh, Mr. Kurt," Joe said, racing back, "my brother and I made an interesting discovery today. Won't you come down to the guest room? I'd like to show it to you."

The headmaster paused and eyed the boy suspiciously. "You're very friendly all of a sudden," he remarked tartly.

"Well, we *are* trying to solve the same mystery, aren't we?" Joe asked disarmingly.

All this time he was trying to figure out just what

to show Kurt which would keep the headmaster occupied while he returned to let Frank out. It would even be better if Greg went back to do it.

"I'm very busy," said Kurt, "but I'll go."

By this time Joe had decided what to tell the headmaster. When the three reached the room, Joe, his back to Kurt, noisily riffled some newspapers in the bureau drawer. But he also was scribbling a note to Greg on the top border of one of them.

"Where is that clipping?" he said aloud, as he wrote:

Tower end of study hall. Push third panel from left. Let Frank out.

After quickly tearing off the note and wadding it, Joe gave the newspaper a final rattle, then turned around.

"Mr. Kurt, I'm afraid your cleaning woman tidied up altogether too well. But," he added, passing in front of Greg and pushing the note into his hand, "if you can spare a few more minutes, I'll tell you the gist of what we discovered."

Greg arose. "Guess you two don't need me. I have to make a phone call," he said.

When he had left, Joe said slowly and with great emphasis, "We Hardys saw a printed article that gave us an idea. There's a gold mine named the Yellow Feather!"

If Joe had tried to wring a confession from Kurt he could not have chosen a better method. The man jumped out of the chair on which he had been waiting impatiently, his face ash white.

"You—you— Where did you see that?" he exclaimed. "A newspaper? Let me see it at once. Oh, you said the cleaning woman had thrown it out. I must have it at once. I'll look in the trash. I'll—"

Still muttering incoherently, the headmaster made a beeline for the stairway and disappeared. Joe chuckled softly.

"I didn't say we saw the notice in a *newspaper clipping,* you moneygrubber," he murmured.

Meanwhile, Frank's eyes were bulging at the discovery he had made in the tower's second-floor room which was completely cut off from the lower section. Near the door lay the discarded desk top with the ominous carved words REVENGE HARRIS D.

Using his pocket flashlight, Frank discovered similar messages on the underside. I HATE WOODSON. IT WILL SUFFER SOMEDAY. DILLEAU.

"I see why Kurt wanted to hide this desk top," Frank thought as he beamed the light around the circular room.

There were various sorts of propulsion gadgets and other sinister-looking objects—no doubt inventions of Kurt's. In the pulled-out drawers of an old-fashioned bureau lay a quantity of small yellow feathers and a supply of wigs, beards, and mustaches.

Frank nearly laughed aloud. "I wonder if Kurt's goatee is real," he thought. "I believe I'll have to give it a tug sometime!"

There was a winding staircase leading to the roof, up which Frank climbed gingerly, but there was nothing to be seen at the top except a weatherproof ventilator. Frank spent the rest of the time looking for the will but did not find it. At the end of the ten-minute period he returned to the panel to wait for Joe to let him out. Though Frank was sure he could open it, he did not want to be discovered coming through the secret door.

As he waited, the door suddenly slid back, revealing Greg. "I'll explain everything in a minute," Greg whispered, as Frank stepped through and closed the panel. "Hurry!"

Frank followed obediently and they met Joe in the hall.

"Where's Kurt?" Greg whispered.

"In the cellar. Let's go outdoors where he can't bother us and exchange our stories."

The three boys took a long walk where they could laugh without restraint at the trick they had played on Kurt. But finally they became serious, and after Frank reported that he had not found the missing will, the talk got around to the various unsolved angles of the mystery.

"I have a hunch if we could figure out the meaning of that word *Manitoba*—" Joe said slowly.

But no new ideas occurred to the boys and they returned to the school just as the warning supper bell rang.

"Fifteen minutes to wash," Greg announced.

At supper the Hardys caught Kurt glancing suspiciously at them several times. Did he suspect their ruse?

"We'd better act pretty nonchalant until we shove off for bed," Frank advised.

They remained with the students during the rest of the evening. When the dorm grew quiet and it was apparent that everyone else was asleep, including Greg, the brothers began to talk in whispers about the mysterious connection between Manitoba and the Yellow Feather case.

"If the will wasn't filed up there," Joe said, "I don't understand why old Elias would have emphasized the word in that message."

"Unless it was a connecting link to the next clue." Frank sat up straight in his chair. "You don't suppose—the library! Come on, Joe!"

Without explaining, he led the way on tiptoe down the dimly lighted corridor. Once inside the library he turned on his flashlight.

"We're going to cover this place until we've looked in every book with the word Manitoba in it," he announced.

"Good hunch, Frank. Let's start with the encyclopedia."

"It might be just a word that's circled, or something like that," Frank suggested as they began the task of leafing through every volume that might be expected to contain a reference to the Canadian province.

Several editions of encyclopedias, however, failed to yield a single clue. Next, they started on the geographies.

"I don't see a thing so far," Joe muttered as he flipped through book after book. With Frank holding the small circle of light over the pages, both boys strained their eyes to catch a word or phrase from the masses of print before them.

Finishing one stack of books, Joe began to replace them while Frank, with the light now placed on a table so that its beam spread over a larger area, looked for other possible sources.

"Funny, all these books certainly came out of here," Joe grunted as he tried to squeeze the last one back into the case, "but now I can't seem to get them back in. Oh, for Pete's sake! No wonder— there's another book behind them."

Reaching in, he pulled out a much older volume, dusty and worn. He was about to shove it into place properly when its title caught his eye.

"Frank! Here's one—*Canada: Province by Province.*"

He laid the old volume on the table and flashed the light directly on it as he flipped the book open. As if by magic the heading *Manitoba* stared at them.

And there inserted between the pages was an old, once-white but now yellowed envelope!

With fingers shaking from excitement, Frank picked it out of the book. Joe held the flashlight close as his brother pulled back the unsealed flap. The legal document within was unfolded. The boys gasped.

" 'Last Will and Testament,' " read Joe in a husky whisper, " 'of Elias Woodson!' "

"We've found it!" Frank whispered exultantly.

Placing the valuable document flat on the table with the light close above it, they eagerly scanned the legal terminology. Near the bottom of the second page was the important item.

" 'And to my nephew, Gregory Woodson,' " Frank read, " 'I give and bequeath the balance of my estate including the Woodson Academy, grounds, buildings, and institution, and the Yellow Feather Gold Mine in Colorado.' "

"Greg gets it all!" Joe cheered as loud as he dared, while Frank checked quickly through the rest of the will.

Both boys were so excited about Greg Woodson's good fortune that neither of them heard the slight shifting of feet behind them. Without warning a voice hissed in their ears:

"Oh, no, he doesn't! But thanks for solving the mystery!"

Henry Kurt!

As the boys spun around to confront the man, they felt a fine spray cover their faces. The next instant, Frank and Joe sank unconscious to the library floor!

Some time later, in total darkness, Frank struggled in a daze to pull what felt like a blanket away from his face. Suddenly, wide awake, he sat bolt upright to discover that he was lying on the hard, cold ground! The blanket felt rough and coarse.

It was pitch black and freezing cold. Shivering and chattering, Frank struggled to his feet. Now he remembered the voice in the library and the thin, fine spray that had hit him and Joe in the face.

"Joe!" he muttered weakly. "Where's Joe?"

As if in answer, his toe hit something soft, and he almost fell over it. Kneeling in the blackness, he found a blanketed figure and a moment later the figure stirred.

"Joe!"

"What happened?" Joe asked foggily.

Tersely, Frank reminded him of the whispered threat in the library and the spray that apparently had knocked them both out.

"But where are we?" Joe asked weakly.

"I have no idea," Frank replied. It was so black that he could not even see his brother's face.

When Joe had revived enough to stand, they began to feel their way around in the place where they were confined. All they found was a rough, hard, cold wall enclosing them. A horrible realization began to dawn on Frank.

"I hope I'm wrong," he groaned, "but I'm afraid we're sealed inside Kurt's ice fort—the one the boys made."

CHAPTER XXV

The Final Roundup

"WE'LL never escape!" Joe's cry echoed in the tomb-like enclosure.

The boys seemed to be in a hopeless dilemma. Because they had inspected the fort so carefully only that day, they knew it would be impossible to claw their way through those three-foot walls of solid ice. Kurt had done his evil work well.

Suddenly Frank remembered one possibility. "The entrance! It can't be frozen as hard as the rest of the wall—not yet, anyway!"

It was their only hope. On hands and knees the brothers circled their small prison until they found the faint outline of the doorway.

"Good thing he didn't pack this as thick as the rest of the wall," Frank chattered when he found an indentation in the solid ice.

With numbed hands, and using Joe's pocketknife,

they took turns digging at the rock-hard surface. It was torturous work. Every minute the air seemed to become staler and breathing became more difficult.

They had dug part of a tiny tunnel, little wider than their own fists, when the knife suddenly penetrated the last bit of outside wall.

"We're through!" Joe exulted but in a feeble voice. "And it's morning."

Desperately, Frank scraped and scraped until he had enlarged the small opening to fist size. A blast of fresh air came whistling through, and breathing was noticeably easier.

"We may freeze, but we won't suffocate," Joe said, shivering.

"Maybe we can dig a hole large enough to squeeze through," Frank said hopefully.

Their joy was short-lived; for, just as Frank started to dig again, the pocketknife blade snapped in two! Its other blades were too small to be of any use.

"The only thing we can do now is shout, and hope someone hears us," Frank declared.

Taking turns, they began to yell for help through the narrow opening. There was no reply.

Back at the school, Greg, at this very moment, was talking on the telephone. His voice was worried and excited.

"Hello, Chet?" he cried into the mouthpiece. "You'd better come out here, quick! The Hardys have disappeared. . . . I don't know. But I did see

Kurt sneaking back into the school just after dawn, and I suspect something's up. Benny and I . . . Yes, he's okay now, he's on our side. . . . Neither one of us can find Frank and Joe.''

At Chet's promise to drive out immediately, Greg rushed back to his room to put on outdoor clothes again.

Where could the Hardys be? The question ran round and round in Greg's mind while he impatiently awaited the arrival of Chet. When the youth arrived, it was in his father's old farm truck.

"I borrowed this," Chet yelled over the noise of the motor as he hurried up to the door, "so I could bring my propeller sled. We can cover more ground on it."

They lifted the sled from the truck and Chet started the motor without any waste of time, while Greg parked the farm vehicle.

"Where do we go first?" Chet asked.

"Let's try the woods," Greg suggested, running back and jumping on the sled.

As they bounced along one of the trails, Chet noticed the ice fort.

"What's that?" he asked.

"Something Kurt had the fellows build yesterday. Oh, good night, the doorway's sealed up!" Greg cried as they neared the fort. "It had an opening yesterday! You don't suppose—"

"Looks as if someone had cut a small hole through the wall, though," Chet remarked as he stopped the sled. He hopped off, placed his mouth near the open-ing, and shouted:

"Frank! Joe! Hey, anybody inside?"

There was no answer. Did this mean no one was there, or that one or more persons within had suc-cumbed to the cold?

"We must break through that wall!" Greg cried. "We'll get picks and crowbars."

"And waste too much time," Chet said. "If Frank and Joe are in there, we must get them out pronto!"

"But how?"

"I have it!" Chet announced. "I spent all day yes-terday fixing this gimmick. Look out!"

Bouncing back onto the propeller sled, he put the gears into reverse. Then hastily he backed the sled to the wall of the fort. With the propellers spinning so that their sharp edges cut into the hard ice, he backed the sled harder and harder against the wall.

"It's biting the ice away!" Greg cried. "You'll be through it in a minute!"

Chunks and fragments of ice flew in all directions. Suddenly the last of the barrier gave way, and Chet had to kill the engine with a lightning thrust of his hand so that the sled would not push right into the enclosure.

Greg was already peering inside. Two blanketed figures lay motionless on the ground.

"Frank and Joe!" he exclaimed, terror in his voice.

Chet looked at his friends' still bodies a second, then sprang into action.

"We must get them out of here!" Chet's voice was shaky. "Oh, it just can't be too late!"

The brothers were carried out into the pale warmth of the winter morning sun. Frank and Joe were still breathing. With Greg and Chet giving first aid, the Hardys quickly recovered consciousness. Feebly Frank murmured:

"Arrest Kurt!"

"You attend to that, Greg," Chet ordered. "I'll bring the boys. It'll have to be a slow, easy ride."

Greg waited long enough to help bundle Frank and Joe aboard the sled, then he raced off on foot. Halfway to the school he met Benny Tass.

"Where you running?" the boy asked.

Forgetting that Benny might still be loyal to Kurt, Greg blurted out the story of the near-fatal kidnaping of the brothers. All the color drained from Benny's face.

"Have you seen Kurt?" Greg demanded.

"A little while ago," Benny answered. "He asked me where you and Chet were going, and I told him you were looking for the Hardys."

"Come on. We're going to his room," Gregg commanded.

But the headmaster was not there. Greg and Benny rushed from one end of the school to the other without finding any trace of the missing man. They concluded that he must have realized the net was closing in around him and had fled.

As they finished their search, Chet slowly maneuvered the sled to the main entrance. Willing hands helped move the Hardy boys into the school infirmary on the third floor. Fortunately, the nurse had returned from her vacation.

"They'll be all right, with some treatment and rest," she said, relieving everyone's mind.

Before the Hardys went to sleep, they were assured that the police had been alerted by Greg to be on the lookout for Kurt who probably was the wanted Harris Dilleau and had quickly left Woodson when arrest seemed imminent.

By the next morning, neither of the Hardys was any the worse for his harrowing experience, and the police came to take full statements from both boys. Since Kurt had not been found, Frank and Joe insisted upon lending a hand. Besides capturing the criminal, they were determined to recover the will!

As Greg and Chet came to the infirmary door, they met the brothers just coming out. In their haste the Hardys ran full tilt into their friends.

"Thought you were sick," Chet gasped, recovering his balance.

"Come on with us!" Joe cried. "We think we know where Kurt is!"

To Chet's and Greg's amazement, the Hardys went only to the second floor, then disappeared into the study hall. Frank pushed back the secret panel and flashed a light inside the dark room. Everyone peered in. The place was still and empty.

"Kurt's not here," Joe announced in disappointment.

But Frank's sharp eyes had noticed a pile of rugs which had not been there the day before. Stepping into the room, he lifted the rugs to reveal a crouching figure beneath.

The wily headmaster!

Kurt never had a chance to move. He was surrounded and yanked to his feet by the four husky boys. Still defiant, the man tried to shake them off, asking what right they had to apprehend him.

"You answer that," Frank said.

His hand stabbed into the man's inside coat pocket as Kurt struggled and cursed.

"The will!" Frank cried gleefully as he retrieved the envelope. Handing it to Greg, he said, "Your grandfather left his entire estate to you!"

Greg was too dumfounded to speak. As Joe told him how they had found the document, only to have it snatched from them, they pointed out the vital paragraphs.

"How can I ever repay you?" the happy heir cried. "Money could never make up for risking your lives to help me."

The brothers smiled. "Don't try," they said in unison. "We like catching criminals."

Kurt, completely beaten, confessed everything the Hardys had suspected about his nefarious efforts to deprive Greg of his rightful inheritance.

In desperation he had had the ice fort built, hoping to imprison the Hardys in it.

"I'm Dilleau," he admitted. "When I was a student here, I was caught stealing. Elias Woodson gave me a tongue-lashing, for which I have hated him ever since. I determined to get revenge and tried to sell some of his valuable books, but he found me out and I was expelled."

Kurt went on to say that he planned for years to come back and be headmaster—maybe even succeed in taking the school away from its owner. But, in the meantime, he ran afoul of the law and had spent some time in prison.

"I escaped," the man explained. "Then I had my face operated on and grew this goatee. When I came back here, Woodson didn't recognize me. I showed him some phony papers and sold him the idea of giving me the job of assistant headmaster. I had a lot of theatrical gear and used to disguise myself to do a little thievery.

"Old man Woodson made the mistake of telling me about that gold mine and I resolved to get hold of it. One evening I saw his will and knew I would have to destroy it. But Mr. Woodson was clever—I'll give him credit for that. He took the will out of his desk and hid it."

Kurt then told how, the night before Woodson's death, the old man had laughed and said he was devising a puzzle so that no one could steal the estate from his grandson.

"I surprised Woodson in the library making a sheet with cutouts," Kurt said. "Just then a student called me. When I got back, the paper was gone and the old man was lying in a faint. He died that night. Later I learned he had tossed a letter out the window with the paper in it."

"And you found the cutout sheet on the river?" Frank asked him.

"Yes. I thought it would throw your father and everyone else off the track if I made a fake one and said Mr. Woodson had given it to me."

Presently plain-clothes men came to arrest Kurt. They planned to keep him at Bayport headquarters until the authorities of the prison from which he had escaped arrived to take charge. He signed a full statement which the four boys read and talked about the rest of the day.

Chet was sure nothing so exciting would ever happen to the Hardys and himself again, but he was wrong, as he learned when he became involved in the boys' next mystery, **THE CLUE OF THE HOODED HAWK.**

But right now he wanted to learn every detail of *The Yellow Feather Mystery*. Since Benny Tass and Skinny Mason already knew so much about the case, they were called in to hear the details.

"Kurt was the one who knocked Joe out at the cabin while you were asleep, Benny," Frank said. "He waited until my brother went outside for wood, then slugged him. Kurt hid Joe's skis and dragged him off to the boathouse. He got back before you woke up."

As Benny, conscience-stricken, looked down at the floor, Greg took up the story. "Kurt was the one who put the poison in my coffee and then stuck a yellow feather under the cup to scare me."

Benny became more and more ashamed. "To think I fell for that stuff about the Yellow Feather!" he groaned.

"We all did," Greg said.

Young Woodson told Benny that he was convinced Kurt's warped sense of humor was partly responsible. The headmaster had apparently enjoyed leading him on about the Yellow Feather with a play on the words *miner* and *minor*.

"Another one of his jokes," Frank stated, "was jimmying the lock on his own office door, so that he could plant my scarf there."

"Kurt probably hastened my grandfather's death with exaggerations about the bad financial conditions here at the school," Greg remarked. "And he tried to scare me off with a lot of phony threats and letters."

"But how about the time Chet was knocked out in the tool shed?" Benny inquired.

"Kurt did that, too," Frank replied, "with a dart from one of his propulsion guns. And he fired harpoons at us from Rocky Point."

"And remember the time we got the yearbook back from you," Joe could not resist needling Tass.

"That same night Kurt was prowling around our house. Dad saw him and barely missed catching him."

"I'm sorry I ever got mixed up with him," Benny said. "I've learned my lesson, fellows. Say, I wonder if Kurt was the one who made me get off that ladder the night I started to climb to your room."

"No," said a voice familiar to the Hardy boys. They turned to see their father standing in the doorway. "As a matter of fact," Mr. Hardy went on, "I was the one."

Grinning, the famous detective told Benny that for a few minutes he had thought the ladder climber was the Yellow Feather.

"Me!" Benny exclaimed.

Frank introduced his father to Greg Woodson, who thanked him and his sons for their clever detective work.

Mr. Hardy smiled. "The case was an unusual one," he said. "Coming back to my old school to work on a mystery and then learning that a secret entrance to the tower had been built was exciting in itself." He turned to his sons. "Mr. Woodson's old friend in Winnipeg told me this. I was afraid the Yellow Feather might imprison one of you in the tower."

He suddenly laughed heartily. "Do you know," he added, "this is the first time a jail breaker ever came to me as Kurt did and asked me to help him catch himself!"

"So there wasn't really any Yellow Feather after all," Chet spoke up.

"Except the mine," the detective said. "Greg, it's not worked out yet. There's plenty of gold left. That mine is a very valuable one."

Greg's eyes glistened. "I'll go out there after graduation. Want to come along, fellows?"

There was a chorus of "Do we!"